The Age of Lead
and Other Fantastic
Romances

The Age of Lead and Other Fantastic Romances

by
Henri Falk

translated by
Brian Stableford

A Black Coat Press Book

ISBN 978-1-935558-42-2. First Printing. August 2010. Published by Black Coat Press, an imprint of Hollywood Comics.com, LLC, P.O. Box 17270, Encino, CA 91416.

Table of Contents

Introduction 7

THE ASTONISHING ADVENTURE OF SÉBASTIEN
PHLIPOT... 17

THE MASTER OF THE THREE STATES 55

THE AGE OF LEAD.. 139

Introduction

Little biographical information regarding Henri Falque (1881-1937), who signed almost all his published writings Henri Falk, is recoverable from contemporary sources, save for the dates of his birth and death, and what little can be inferred from the record of his publications. The earliest of these was a dissertation on *Les Privilèges de librairie sous l'Ancien Régime* [Bookstores Privileges under the French Monarchy] (1906), which was presumably written to obtain some academic or professional qualification, perhaps in law. Studying law was the traditional reserve strategy of many would-be French writers, and Falk would have been following a well-trodden path had he taken some such qualification while attempting to get a writing career off the ground.

We can assume that his early writings were very various. Three of the longer stories assembled in his first, self-published, collection of prose items are individually dated, the inscriptions ranging from September 1906 to September 1908, and it is possible that the other, significantly shorter pieces, were written to round out the volume, which appeared as *Le Cadre volé* [The Stolen Frame] in 1910. *Le Porte-cartes* [The Card-Case], the first of several one-act comedies he published before the outbreak of the Great War, was issued in the same year, and a volume entitles *Poèmes brefs, idylles et comédies* [Short Poems, Idylls and Comedies] followed in 1911. His second story-collection, *La Main d'or* [The Golden Hand] (1913), consists entirely of short pieces tailored for newspaper publication, all of them deliberately trivial; 11 stories in the collection are placed in a subset titled "*contes fantaisistes*" [fanciful tales], but none of the stories it contains are fantastic, most being whimsical anecdotes. Falk's first collection, on the other hand, contained two long stories with fantastic inclinations, one of which, "L'Etonnante aventure de Sébastien Phlipot" (here translated as "The Astonishing Adventure of Sébastien Phlipot"), is a full-blown historical fantasy, which borders on scientific romance by virtue of its careful, if comic, extrapolation of a notion popularized by the late 19th century boom in "psychic research" and here transplanted to the context of the "animal magnetism" fad initiated in Paris by Anton Mesmer in the 1780s.

Although Falk seems to have built up a thriving career as an author of one-act comedies, and had begun to dabble in full-length comedy by 1914, when *Les Agités* [The Disturbed] was published, it was decisively interrupted by the war. He was almost certainly mobilized as soon as the war began, and probably remained in military service until its end. This did not, however, entirely put a stop to his writing. Publication opportunities for any kind of fiction, especially comedy, were very thin on the ground for the first few years of the war, but they began to broaden out again in 1917, when Falk published a two-part novella in the *Mercure de France* entitled "Le Maître des trois états" (here translated as "The Master of the Three States"). Although it is an archetypical example of what Maurice Renard had called "*le roman merveilleux-scientifique*" [scientific marvel fiction], it is more broadly comic than most stories of that sort, and has some affinities with the kind of darkly farcical intrusive fantasy popularized in Victorian England by F. Anstey [Thomas Anstey Guthrie] in such works as *Vice*

Versa (1882) and *The Fallen Idol* (1886), a coarser version of which had been revived in England during the war by W. A. Darlington in the stories subsequently collected in *Alf's Button* (*Passing Show* 1917-18; book 1919), when the authorities belatedly came round to the view that a little laughter was not merely permissible in terrible times, but might actually be good for morale.

When the war ended, and Falk returned to civilian life, he went back to the theater and produced more comedies, as well as song-lyrics and librettos for operettas. The play that was eventually to prove his most popular and influential, the flirtatious romance *Pouche*, was written in collaboration with René Peter, first produced in 1923, then published the following year. It owes its modern fame to an English translation by Avery Hopwood, *Naughty Cinderella* (produced 1925; published 1934), which was adapted into the film *This is the Night* (1932). Alongside his theatrical work, however, Falk produced numerous prose pieces. Those that appeared in volume form included an illustrated novelette in the same genre as "Le Maître des trois états," *L'Age de Plomb* (here translated as "The Age of Lead"), which appears to have been written shortly after the end of the war, although the book is undated and bibliographical notations merely offer the guess that it was published *circa* 1922.

By 1922, as the introductions to the Black Coat Press collections of the works of Maurice Renard and J.-H. Rosny Aîné explain, scientific romance had fallen into extreme disfavor in the French literary marketplace, and it is not surprising that Falk, like almost everyone else who had dabbled in the genre, gave up on it. His subsequent novels are all naturalistic. In the years preceding his somewhat premature death, he did some

9

scriptwriting work for French films, and some of his own works were used as the bases for film scripts, but he made no considerable impact in that or any other arena. Some bibliographies list an undated collection of *Contes et nouvelles extr. de la presse,* but it is extremely elusive and I have no idea what it contains. There was a posthumous reissue of "Le Maître des trois états" in 1939 under the title of *La Fantastique invention de César Pitoulet,* credited to Falk and Paul Plançon, but that, too, is elusive, and I do not know whether it was revised from the *Mercure de France* version—the latter being the one that I have translated—or why Plançon's name was added, if that was not the reason.

All in all, the author remains something of a mystery.

Slender though it is—unless other relevant works remain to be discovered—Falk's contribution to the development of French scientific romance is by no means trivial. The first two works reprinted here are quite striking, and although the third is weaker, it is by no means uninteresting. The quality of the comedy therein is quite distinct, although it carries forward a long tradition of sardonically humorous speculative fiction, constituted by the relevant works of Villiers de l'Isle-Adam Charles Cros, Alphonse Allais, Didier de Chousy, Alfred Jarry and Gaston de Pawlowski, among others.[1]

The first two stories included here feature a risqué element that, although carefully restrained and rather

---

[1] The following works are available in Black Coat Press editions: *The Scaffold* and *The Vampire Soul* by Villiers de l'Isle-Adman; *Ignis* by Didier de Cousy; *Journey to the Land of the Fourth Dimension* by Gaston de Pawlowski.

elliptical, was unusual for the time, and which bears some slight resemblance to the series of Americanized Ansteyan fantasies that Thorne Smith subsequently produced, beginning with *Topper* (1926) and *The Stray Lamb* (1929). Although elements of the basic theme of "L'Etonnante aventure de Sébastien Phlipot" were occasionally recapitulated in later fantastic fiction, few—if any—of the later treatments pay such interested attention to the complexities introduced into the protagonist's sex life by his peculiar circumstances.

"L'Etonnante aventure de Sébastien Phlipot," which is dated September 1908 in *Le Cadre volé*, obviously owes something to the research into the *Ancien Régime* that Falk carried out for the benefit of his dissertation, and also seems to reflect a genuine, if thoroughly skeptical, interest in the products of French psychic research. Presumably, he found the idea for the story in the book by Colonel de Rochas that he cites in the note appended to the end of the novelette, but the fact that he chooses to project it back in time to the heyday of "animal magnetism" has several beneficial effects, not least the fact that it emphasizes the special significance contained in the word *sensibilité*, which I have translated as "sensibility" rather than "sensitivity" in honor of the particular popularization given to the term by Jean-Jacques Rousseau.

Although not an empiricist himself, Rousseau was one of the contributors to the *Encyclopédie* whose empiricist philosophy provides a key element of the story's philosophical background, and his affirmation of the nobility of human sentiments uncorrupted by civilization spawned a "cult of sensibility" that produced many literary echoes, both sincere and sardonic.

Rousseau is not mentioned in "L'Etonnante aventure de Sébastien Phlipot," and nor is Voltaire (although

11

one of the latter's most significant places of publication is cited), but their presence in spirit is undeniable; the story is set firmly in the tradition of sarcastic *contes philosophiques* founded by the later, which includes the founding text of French scientific romance, *Micromégas* (1752). As with many other works looking slyly back at Rousseau's eccentric contribution to the French Romantic tradition, Falk's story develops a contest between sense and sensibility that favors the former, while admitting the attractions of the latter. Falk's portrait of a hypothetical innocent unfortunately separated from his sensibility offers little support for Rousseau's thesis regarding the roots of human virtue in its deft extrapolation of Phlipot's predicament. If the story is not as polished as Voltaire's *contes philosophiques*—as very few later examples are—it certainly does not fall short in offering food for thought, wittily and unassumingly, along with a healthy dose of pure entertainment.

"Le Maître des trois états" might well have been written as an exercise in psychological self-medication, to give Falk something else to think about instead of the horrors and terrors of the war rather than as a commercial exercise, and it is a rather surprising piece to find in the pages of the *Mercure de France*, in spite of Alfred Vallette's apparent covert sympathy for "scientific marvel fiction." An official organ of the Symbolist movement in its early years, the *Mercure* had gradually become conscientiously staid and respectable, and was well into its maturity by 1917, but "Le Maître des trois états" probably went down better with its readers than the other major piece of French scientific marvel fiction published in 1917 (a review of which appears in the *Mercure*'s pages immediately after the concluding part of Falk's serial), J.-H. Rosny Aîné's *L'Enigme de Gi-*

vreuse [2] would have done. It is much more coherent and faster-paced, as well as funnier. The fact that it is set in the weeks immediately preceding the war lends it a slightly nostalgic tint, but adds an unusually wry note to the hapless scientist's final speech anticipating potential future applications of his ironically-doomed invention.

The closest relatives of "Le Maître des trois états" in French scientific romance are the stories in a series of accounts of eccentric scientific inventions that André Couvreur wrote for *Oeuvres Libres* between 1922 and 1939, following on from *Une invasion de microbes*, which had appeared in a different publication in 1909. Falk might well have read the last-named story, just as Couvreur probably read "Le Maître des trois états." Although the effects of César Pitoulet's Great Transmutator are purely fantastic, like the inventions pioneered by Couvreur's Professor Tornada, there is a telling conscientiousness about their extrapolation, even when played for laughs, which exploits the gloss of plausibility typical of classic scientific marvel fiction in order to add a valuable *conte philosophique* element to the story.

L'Age de Plomb is a disaster story reminiscent in its basic schema of J.-H. Rosny Aîné's *La Force mystérieuse* (1913),[3] but blatantly farcical in its development; it is presumably by design that the scientist who solves the enigma of the global plague has the same surname as the teller of tall stories who features in several items in the *contes fantaisistes* section of *Le Main d'or*. Farcical as it is, however, *L'Age de Plomb* is clearly a

---

[2] Translated in a Black Coat Press edition as *The Givreuse Enigma and Other Stories.*
[3] Translated in a Black Coat Press edition as *The Mysterious Force and Other Anomalous Phenomena),*

product of post-war consciousness, and the final judgment that it passed on the disaster once it has abated is markedly different from the judgments passed on similar temporary catastrophes in such pre-war works as *La Force mystérieuse* and Arthur Conan Doyle's *The Poison Belt*, and can obviously be read as a reflection on the war itself. It is not the direct effects of the malign influence that slows civilization down to a crawl, but the weight of the armor that people have to adopt in order to ward it off, and the consequent drastic narrowing of social horizons, and there is not the slightest suggestion that any worthwhile moral lesson has been learned from the ordeal.

L'Age de Plomb has none of the peculiar eccentricities exhibited in "L'Etonnante aventure de Sébastien Phlipot" and "Le Maître des trois états," and is thus placed much closer to the mainstream of French comic fiction, although connoisseurs of eccentricity are bound to regret the lack. One could easily believe it to be the work of a different hand—and perhaps it was, in the sense that Falk, like many other ex-combatants, probably did not come out of the war the same man that he went in. Nor did he ever return in his literary work to the wryly inquisitive consciousness that produced his earlier scientific romances.

Perhaps this was because he, like the editors who swiftly reduced the aspiring stream of post-war French scientific romance to a sickly trickle, shared the general disenchantment with the produce of science prompted by the technical sophistication of arms and armament that the war had provoked, or perhaps he simply wanted to lighten up and have some uninhibited fun. Either way, there is reason for lovers of speculative fiction to be glad that he did produce the works assembled here, all of which retain their readability today.

Brian Stableford

THE ASTONISHING ADVENTURE OF SÉBASTIEN PHLIPOT

Do not to dare to speak harshly to someone accused
of a sin of the heart.
Montaigne
Essais: "On the Art of Discussion"

The following story is extracted *verbatim* from the papers of Jean-Pierre-Sébastien Phlipot. The editor owes their obliging communication to Monsieur Jacques-François Phlipot, the last of that name, who reserves for the time being the right to publish his ancestor's memoirs in full.

(Folio 17, page 1)

I, Jean-Pierre Sébastien Phlipot, aged 36, spouse of Jeanne-Marie Lamitié, happy father of a loving daughter, honorable herbalist keeping a shop on the Rue Saint-Honoré bearing the sign *Palm Oils*, virtuous citizen, rational, worthy of belief, desire to record here an astonishing adventure, more admirable than a tale by Galland and as real as the pen that is retracing it, of which I was the hero, in Paris, the hearth of enlightenment and philosophy, in the year of grace 1784.

It is well-known that, for more than five years, in the city as well as the court, there has been talk of nothing but "electricity" and "animal magnetism." Everyone is intellectually infatuated with the practices of Mesmer, Puységur and Cagliostro.[4] That is the current fashion. These gentlemen are fêted everywhere, in the theater and in drawing-rooms, the Saint-Germain fair and the Rue Bergère. I suspect that the widowed Madame Geoffrin, my severe neighbor and constant visitor, has never received them, as Necker[5] did, but does anyone know where we are headed? A whirlwind drives us toward

---

[4] Anton Mesmer (1734-1815) had arrived in Paris in 1778, having left Vienna under a cloud, and his medical treatments employing "animal magnetism" swiftly became a topic of immense controversy. The Marquis de Puységur (1751-1825) was one of his most ardent disciples; it was one of Puységur's "subjects"—probably acting on his own initiative—who began going into a kind of trance when hypnotized, thus popularizing "artificial somnambulism." The Italian charlatan who called himself Count Cagliostro, who had already built a reputation as a magician and fortune-teller, was drawn into the controversy by apparent association. 1784 was a crucial year for Mesmer because Louis XVI ordered the establishment of a scientific committee to determine whether there really was a bodily "magnetic fluid" of the kind that Mesmer claimed; its members included Antoine Lavoisier, Benjamin Franklin and the astronomer Jean-Sylvain Bailly, and it delivered a negative report. The same year saw the famous scandal of the "Affair of the Necklace," in which Cardinal de Rohan was conned out of a large amount of money with the aid of a masquerader pretending to be Marie-Antoinette; although Cagliostro was almost certainly uninvolved, he was called to testify in the trial (in 1786) and subsequently expelled from France.
[5] Jacques Necker (1732-1804), the former finance minister, had retired from that position by 1784, although he was subsequently recalled in a doomed attempt to rescue the nation's finances before, during and after the Revolution on 1789.

new ideas; one flies from one surprise to the next—and I have had my share of surprises!

As one might imagine, Mesmer and Cagliostro have given rise to a host of emulators. It is for that reason that, last August, a magnetizer came to lodge nearby, in the Rue des Poulies. The news spread more rapidly than quicksilver. From the Quai Bourbon to the Oratoire, there was solemn talk of marvels: he put people to sleep by gazing at them in a certain way, healed wounds and cured pains with certain gestures.

In the first rank of gossips, my wife shone. While crushing my herbs in the laboratory, I heard her chattering away in the shop—and 20 times a day she came in to tell me that Signor Palestrino had just cured, in a matter of minutes, a young woman with a pale complexion, that he promised to become the greatest sorcerer in the realm, that the entire neighborhood was rushing to see his experiments, and that it was extremely nasty and inglorious on my part to deprive a faithful spouse of the pleasure of admiring them.

One always ends up giving in to women; one might as well do so at the start and avoid a great deal of annoyance. So, on August 17 last, at 4 p.m., I booked two 40-*sou* seats for the evening session. At 7 p.m., therefore, after dinner, we were ready to set off—but Louison, ordinarily very calm, sobbed so mightily on seeing us leave that Mariette, war-weary, picked her up. The child stopped crying, and I did not doubt that free admission would be given to a two-year-old child, gentle and well-behaved, carried by her mother.

We arrived at the Rue des Poulies. On the third floor of a dilapidated house, a little lackey took our tickets and showed us, along with Louison, into a large, rather poorly-lit room whose walls were hung with red cloth, overheated by a numerous audience—so we were glad to be shown to two seats near the open window.

Palestrino was late. To kill time, some members of the audience were examining an empty armchair on a dais in the middle of the room, while others were chatting in hushed voices, some calling the Italian a rogue and others a genius. For myself, I had no fixed opinion, estimating with the gentlemen of the *Dictionnaire* that one cannot be sure of anything until one has tested it for oneself.[6]

Suddenly, he appeared, without anyone having seen him come in. He bowed very politely. He was a little, bony, jaundiced man with keen eyes and black hair. While cracking his knuckles he asked us in a nasal accent whether we were all "believers." Naturally, we said yes. They he summoned a young woman who was standing upright in a corner. "I shall proceed with my first experiment," he said. "Take your place, Mademoiselle Sarah."

The young woman sat down in the armchair in the middle of the dais. He waved his hands around; she sighed and closed her eyes. "I can put her to sleep very quickly," he said, "by virtue of the force of habit."

Then, penetrating into our ranks, he leaned toward each of us in turn, and asked everyone to name an object for him, or give him an instruction, in a low voice. And Mademoiselle Sarah named the object in question or carried out the instruction given. We consulted one another with our gazes, most of us suspecting the use of some secret alphabet between the man and the sleeper.

---

[6] The *Dictionnaire* was an alternative name for the famous *Encyclopédie*, the crucial document of the French Enlightenment, compiled between 1751 and 1772.

He continued, though: "That was only the prelude. Although I have established a *state of rapport* with mademoiselle, it was with a view to another, especially interesting, experiment, which I shall not carry out on her person, but on a member of the learned audience. Mademoiselle Sarah, a good *subject*, if you please!"

Without hesitation, she replied: "The herbalist over there, sitting next to the window."

All eyes turned toward me. Palestrino blew on Mademoiselle Sarah's face, and she woke up, smiling. Then he said to me: "If you please, Monsieur, I will deal with you shortly—but I shall ask first whether anyone in the audience is in pain or feeling ill: that pain, I shall take away, and incorporate it into this"—he took a little ball out of his pocket, which he set on a plate—"and then I shall burn it, and the pain with it."

No one made any reply. However, I saw Père Tilleul, the clockmaker, there, who had been cursing his catarrh that very morning, and Laurent Maclou, who suffers from dropsy.

"I observe with pleasure," the Italian said, ironically, that everybody here is perfectly well." He turned to me: "No infirmity, Monsieur Phlipot? I can cure you more easily than anyone else."

I said to myself then: *This man isn't the Devil. He's just called me by my name; but everyone around here knows me. If he doesn't cure me, he'll be ashamed; if he does cure me, I'll have got my forty* sous' *worth.*

At the same time, Mariette whispered: "Tell him about your rheumatism."

My dialectic, my wife's insistence and a desire to humiliate Maclou—ever a braggart, presently picked in modesty—caused me to reply firmly: "I sometimes have an ache in my shoulder."

"Marvelous," he said. "Take your place." And he pointed at the armchair, where I obligingly sat down.

"Are you in pain this evening?" he asked me.

"No," I said, "but I get it every winter."

"Next winter, you won't suffer again."

He looked at me, placed his hands on my shoulders, suddenly took them away, grasped the ball, kneaded it, then set fire to it and melted it in the flame of a candle.

"You're cured," he said, with a pirouette—but as I got up, he added: "That's not all. This experiment will only have a distant effect, and for the edification of the assembly, I would like to make immediate use of the special faculties of which you are the instrument."

"What do you mean, Monsieur?" I asked.

"You're an ideal subject for my favorite experiment."

"An ideal subject?"

"Don't you experience all sensations of pain or pleasure keenly?"

"I'm quite sensitive and squeamish."

"It's the same thing, my dear Monsieur Phlipot. With your permission, I shall carry out an experiment on you without any danger, but of such interest that you will retain the memory of it as long as you live. Will you permit me to relieve you of your sensibility for a few minutes? I'll give it back to you as soon as you wish. I repeat that the experiment involves no danger."

I turned my eyes toward Mariette—who, as curious as a she-monkey, had no inclination to call me back to her side. An attentive frisson ran through the audience; Maclou smiled, as if certain that I would refuse. Too far committed to retreat, I acquiesced, on condition that I would not be put to sleep.

"You'll remain awake," said the Italian, "and I shall have the joy of explaining all the phases of the experiment to you—for there's no mystery about it. Are you ready?"

What decided me was that "there's no mystery about it." *Here's a man*, I thought, *who addresses himself to understanding, not to credulity.*

"Let's go," I said.

His hands immediately began to move, as if rowing through the air, along my body.

"These," he said—I had time enough afterwards to transcribe his words—"are the passes designed to distribute evenly over the surface of the body the molecules of sensitive fluid that only escape ordinarily through the extremities of the limbs, just as the fluid of a magnet only flows from the tips of its branches."

Meanwhile, he drowned me in the light that poured out of his pupils. I could not tear my eyes away from his, and I felt as if I were dazzled. To the question that I asked mentally, he replied: "It's nothing. Don't speak. Don't think. Don't resist my will."

On these words, although I was awake, I ceased to be the same. Some unfamiliar element, invisible and real, gushed out of me. The Italian slowed down his passes, and, without taking his eyes of me, he said: "Mademoiselle Sarah, a *mumie*!"[7]

---

[7] I have retained Falk's spelling of the word "mumie" rather than substituting the more familiar English equivalent "mummy," just as he deliberately refrains from using the conventional French spelling, *momie*. In fact, "mumie" was used in the title of the first English translation of a book by Paracelsus, *Medicina Diastetica; or, Sympatheticall Mumie* (1653), which is presumably the text that Palestrino will shortly ap-

The young woman held out a little cylinder as long as a thumb, saffron in color, which he swiftly transferred into my hands. I observed that one of the cylinder's ends was rounded off; the material seemed to me to be compounded of wax and gum Arabic; its aroma was similar to that of incense.

At the same time, Palestrino slowly raised his hands, curved into cups, as if he were lifting up a heavy weight.

"Together," he said, "we shall infuse the *mumie*." Then he suddenly blew on my face, passed a hand over my forehead, clicked his tongue, took possession of the cylinder and presented it to me. "Here," he said, "is your sensibility. After bringing it to the surface of your body, I distributed outside in parallel layers of fluid, then concentrated it, and finally incorporated it into this *mumie*."

He fell silent. No one breathed. I was so nonplussed that I dared not interrogate him.

He resumed speaking: "The substance therein is more than adequate to store the sensitive fluid." Setting the cylinder on a table, without any warning, he gave me the hardest pair of slaps that had ever reddened an honest face since the creation of the world. A sentiment of innate honor caused me to leap out of the armchair, but surprise nailed me to the seat again; I had heard the blows that I had just received slap my cheeks sonorous-

propriate as a (misleading) reference. The famous revisionist alchemist and bane of traditional herbalist medicine did suggest various uses for "mumie," the bituminous preservative used in the preservation of Egyptian mummies—which was widely touted by numerous quacks as a treatment for all kinds of ills—but the practice described in the story is not one of them.

ly, *but I had not felt them!* They had made the impression on my skin that a screen suddenly hiding things from view makes on the eye, *but I had not experienced any pain.*

Astonishment doubtless gave my features a comical expression, for the audience burst out laughing.

"Don't bear me any ill-will," said Palestrino. "A blow not felt is not received. From now on, your sensibility is entirely enclosed in this *mumie*."

"That *mumie*?"

"*Mumie* is the name that Paracelsus gave to figurines of this sort. I say figurine, for you'll observe that it broadly mimics the form of the human body. A fine experiment, isn't it? And this is the counter-proof. The slightest touch or pressure exerted upon your *mumie* will give you the sensation to which you would be subject if that touch or pressure had been exercised upon you."

So saying, he pricked the *mumie* in the head; I felt a violent sting in my skull. He squeezed its neck, and I cried: "You're strangling me!" He stopped. I could breathe.

"An imprudence or a bad joke could make you suffer cruelly," he went on. "Have no fear of me—I'm a man of science."

"So much the better, Monsieur!" I replied, very anxiously. "But since it's obvious that the experiment has succeeded, please give me back my sensibility. Only keep my rheumatism!"

My fright had the effect of amusing the audience. There was a stir, and whispers were exchanged. Maclou called me "Sébastien the Magnetic."

Palestrino, however, addressed himself to me. "Thank you, Monsieur," he said, solemnly, "for having confidence in me. You're an intelligent man—and those who are laughing now have not shown your courage. Since that is your desire, I shall return your sensibility to you immediately."

This declaration reassured me. I asked him to entrust the *mumie* to me momentarily, and I did indeed remark that *it felt itself between my fingers*, while my fingers did not feel it at all.

On the insistence of the spectators I got down from the podium and walked among them, with my sensibility in the palm of my hand. Some of them wanted to touch it. I refused, as you may imagine. By way of compensation, I allowed myself to be jabbed, scratched and pinched. Palestrino made me put my index finger over the flame of a candle. As I left it there, tranquilly, he snatched the flame away. "You'll burn yourself all the way to the bone," he told me, "with a smile on your lips."

We all marveled.

"Now," said Palestrino, "we shall reintegrate Mademoiselle Sensibility in her legitimate domicile."

I was, therefore, advancing toward the dais when my wife begged me to entrust the *mumie* to her for a moment. Having no reason to distrust her, I let her caress it at her ease—which made me tingle with pleasure. She was holding out her hand to return it and I was holding out my hand to receive it when our little Louison, doubtless attracted by its bright color, suddenly grabbed the cylinder, shook it frantically, and abruptly opened her hand, emitting a jolly infantile laugh. At the same time, I was seized by vertigo, borne away in a current of air, and completely enveloped a moment thereafter as if by a thick eiderdown.

Palestrino hurled himself forward. On his knees, he searched for the *mumie* beneath my wife's skirts. It was a waste of time. It had vanished.

I was devastated. Everyone had stood up.

"Halt!" cried Palestrino. "You risk crushing Monsieur! Let everyone leave his seat slowly and watch where he puts his feet!"

Everyone obeyed. The audience gathered in one corner of the room. Armed with a torch, the Italian explored the floor, the wall-hangings and the curtains. I helped him as best I could, for I was damp with sweat. Mariette was weeping. It was high time!

Suddenly, striking his forehead, Palestrino pointed to the open window and cried: "There! There! Didn't you feel a violent impact on solid matter?"

"On the contrary," I replied. "I seemed to fall into a warm, soft substance, and I'm steeped in sweat."

He was already leaning out of the window. "Warm and soft!" he exclaimed. "You've had a stroke of luck! Your child threw the *mumie* out of the window, but that heap of dung—can you see it, under the lantern, next to the gutter?—was in exactly the right place to break its fall. Let's go look for it."

He went out in the blink of an eye, and I went after him. He was going through the door to the street and I was still in the middle of the staircase, when I suddenly experienced a cool sensation, and then increasing humidity. Bewildered, and beating the air with my hands, I started shouting: "I'm drowning! I'm drowning!"

Palestrino came back up the steps four at a time when he heard my cries, swore in Italian as soon as he understood their meaning, and went back downstairs at top speed, shouting himself: "The gutter! The gutter!"

I went down after him, with my teeth chattering, sustained by Mariette, and I found him in the street, white with wrath, cursing a neighbor.

"It's that shrew," he cried, "emptying all the slop-pails from her stinking house into the gutter! The heap of dung has come apart, and the *mumie*'s being carried away by the current." Seeing my heartbroken expression, he added: "Fortunately, the current isn't very strong, and we'll doubtless be able to catch up with it soon."

Telling the curious crowd to stand back, he started searching the gutter. He was cursing, I was shivering, Mariette was sobbing and Louise was mewling as we followed its course as far as the end of the street. An unpleasant surprise awaited us there. Originating from the Rue des Fossés-Saint-Germain, a second gutter-stream combined with the first and the two formed a considerable flow of water in the Rue du Petit-Bourbon.

"The worst of it," said Palestrino, letting his hands fall and rebound from his thighs, "is that a third joins the other two level with the Quai de l'Ecole. Their mingled streams pass under the Arche de Bourbon and throw themselves into the Seine level with the Port-au-Blé. *Povero mio!* Good Phlipot, if your *mumie* takes a dive into the river, it will be well and truly lost, and you'll be shivering forever!"

I uttered a despairing wail—but when Mariette uttered one of her own I grabbed her hand forcefully. "God be praised!" I shouted. "It hasn't fallen in! The sensation of dampness is abating. If feel as if I were surrounded by a vast poultice!"

"Hurrah!" said the Italian. "It doesn't require much mental effort to divine that you're stuck in the mud on the bank. The river's low; you're in no danger of being dislodged from your refuge by the water. At this hour, a search is impracticable, but tomorrow at dawn…"

"What do you mean, tomorrow?" I cried. "Must we wait until tomorrow?"

"Don't complain," he said. "Rather think yourself lucky to have lost your *mumie* by night. In broad daylight, it would inevitably have been crushed."

A fit of rage overwhelmed me. I launched myself forward, my fist raised, crying: "Wretch!"

The Italian defended himself, and I can even say that he gave me a thrashing, but I had the advantage of not feeling his blows. Marietta tried to separate us with one arm—Louison was howling in the other. "Listen!" she yelled. "Listen! I've got an idea."

He called a truce in order to hear what she had to say.

"That lady, your Sarah, might be able to indicate the place."

"Alas, good lady Phlipot, Sarah can only read thoughts. She puts herself in rapport with the spirit, not the matter. If your husband asks her what he's thinking, she'll reply: 'About the lost *mumie*.' But as for finding the *mumie*, that she can't do. That's the truth. I'm a man of science."

"Murderer!" I cried, and grabbed him by the collar. "Have no fear, my lad! I'll go to the lieutenant of police! I'll have you locked up tomorrow morning!" But he shoved me to make me let go and fled as fast as his legs could carry him.

I thought that all hope was lost. Furious and desolate, I threw myself on my bed as soon as I got home. I slept badly, in fits and starts. I pinched myself several times, but always without any pain.

Suddenly, I repented of having threatened the Italian. Besides which, he had seemed grieved by the incident. Most of all, I regretted not having asked him whether the destruction of the *mumie* might lead to my death.

As soon as dawn broke, I ran to his house. I knocked—no response.

I made inquiries. He had decamped during the night.

I sat down on a boundary-marker then, and wept.

Suddenly, a street-urchin appeared in front of me, handed me a letter and ran away.

I read:

Phlipot, I don't like violence. Search for the mumie *on your own. If you find it, announce the fact in the personal advertisement section of the* Journal de Paris, *because you will need my services. Save for God, the only person who can return his sensibility to a subject is the operator who extracted it. Palestrino.*

I sat there for a long time, rolling the letter between my fingers, realizing that, in sum, the Italian had not entirely abandoned me. I went back to the house, from which I soon emerged with Mariette, and the 6 a.m. Sun found us squatting on our haunches, beating the mud at the river's edge. We had a little time to ourselves, trying hard not to attract attention—if some bandit took it into his head to imitate us, and found my *mumie* instead of me, to what rightful perils might I be exposed? As I had foreseen, though, half an hour later we were surrounded by a group of curiosity-seekers. To put them off, I secretly buried an *écu*, and having dug it up again cried: "I've found it!" After which we left, with satisfied expressions, and the gawkers went away.

I was impatient to return to the river-bank. While waiting for evening I shut myself away in my room, as much out of chagrin as to get rid of the neighbors who cam incessantly in search of news.

Going out at sunset, Mariette and I resumed our search, but in vain. We came back for dinner when darkness closed in.

Even though my stomach demanded its pittance, meals had become tortures for me. I perceived neither the taste of the foodstuffs nor the aroma of the dishes. The pleasures of the senses no longer existed for me.

That evening, rightly, Mariette gave me a few caresses. Although she was far from awkward, she nevertheless left me stone cold. That, more than anything else, broke my heart. We poor people have not many joys on Earth! And what remains to us, without those of love? Seated on my bed, with my chin on my knees, I bewailed my misery in hot tears. Did I say hot? Alas, I could not feel them running down my cheeks.

In the morning, I did not have the courage to return to the water's edge. I remained cloistered in my room, even though the shop was never empty any longer. The story had spread...

Three days after that evil evening, I was plunged in the blackest thoughts, when Mariette abruptly opened my door and said, breathlessly: "Sébastien, my love, do you know who's downstairs? A lady from the court, a marquis and a medical gentleman, who want to see you and admire you. There's a coach and two chaises in the street, and the neighbors are at their windows."

I protested that I had made my decision, which was not to see anyone, but she persisted. "People of the court, my love!"

I gave in—flattered, I confess, for my part, that the nobility was beating a path to my shop.

As I came in, a young lord, clad in silk, perfumed and powdered, hastened to meet me. "My dear Phlipot!" he said. "I am the Chevalier de Guelinen, and I do you the honor of introducing you to the Marquise d'Armoise."

"And I," said the other visitor, who was older, wore no sword and was dressed in black, "am Doctor Bailli. I'm preparing a report on the hypothesis of magnetic fluid and the phenomena that appear to derive therefrom." He turned to the Marquise, and added: "I say 'appear' for I attribute their origin to pure imagination. This fellow thinks that he doesn't feel anything but in reality…"

"Monsieur," I said, offended, "do you take me for a maniac?" And I narrated my adventure.

The Marquise honored me with a pinch. The Chevalier punched me on the nose. The doctor talked about cutting off one of my fingers to assure himself of my sincerity. "All this," he said, "is scarcely scientific. I shall proceed, however, purely out of scrupulousness, to examine the mud on the river bank. Expect me tomorrow morning."

"We must show you off at court," the Chevalier said to me.

"That's too great an honor," Mariette replied.

When they had gone, she threw herself into my arms. "At court, my love! Our fortune is made!"

I shoved her away, crying: "Bad wife! You'd be pleased, for love of money, to see me deprived forever…"

A lackey came in, who gave me a purse on behalf of the Marquise, containing ten louis and 24 *livres*. The quarrel stopped there.

Bailli came back the next morning, armed with a permission to enclose the area of the search, and we set off, followed by his aides, who set out to dig in the mud in the places I indicated. They worked zealously, not neglecting any section of ground, unearthing a host of debris, and also stout mud-worms, of which the ducks on the river are extremely fond. These impudent creatures came right up to our feet in order to catch the worms.

Meanwhile, Bailli carried out frequent and various experiments on me. He was in the process of pulling out my hair when I felt myself gripped, as if by a vice; the pain was so intense that I collapsed. He picked me up and his aides supported me. The great pain ceased; I thought I was lying inside a pipe.

I confided in Bailli, who replied: "Admit it! All these absurd impressions are purely a product of your imagination!"

"No," I told him, "I won't admit that. I'm sure that your aides have displaced my *mumie* while disturbing the mud. Being so small, it must have escaped your sight—but I would have perceived it, if you hadn't been pulling out my hair. It's doubtless buried in another layer of mud now, contact with which imposes the sensation that I've described to your incompetence!"

He started. "Incompetence!"

The discussion poisoned, he turned his back to me, and I turned mine on him, and limped back home in a pitiful state. A tempest shook me, between walls that seemed to be elastic, hard, warm and moving, all that the same time. At times, I was inundated by cold liquid, doubtless due to an infiltration of the river. At other times, innumerable masses of warm, soft and sticky bodies slid along my body. The continuous shaking, and the alternative sweats and shivers, gave me a violent nausea, complicated by an intense fever. I went to bed.

A few hours later, I was visited by the Chevalier. "Excuse me," he said, "for coming up to see you. I only came to tell you that a court coach will bring you to the Tuileries tomorrow, with your wife, if it pleases you."

"Alas, Monsieur le Chevalier," I replied, "you find me in a very sorry state."

"Can nothing relieve you?"

"I need Palestrino."

"Where's his lair?"

"He's run away. I threatened him with the police."

"Nothing is lost," said the Chevalier. "The lieutenant of police is a friend of mine. Two of his bloodhounds…"

"No!" I cried. "The Italian will certainly put them off the track. Rather let him know that no one will trouble him. If you would please insert in the personal advertisements of the *Journal de Paris*…"

Having listened to me at length, the Chevalier said "Count on me, old chap!" and set off for the newspaper's offices.

I spent the night in the same cruel torment. After dozing off toward morning, I woke up to see Palestrino standing before me.

"I read the advertisement," he said. "I never left the neighborhood. Although you mistreated me, I never stopped thinking about you. I've thought of a means of returning your sensibility to you—it will be sufficient for someone else to consent to give you his."

"Not before tonight, at any rate," said Mariette.

"Be reassured, my good Madame Phlipot—it won't be easy to find that someone…unless you…it's a means of combining vanity with love…you only need to abandon to your dear spouse…"

I started laughing, in spite of everything, as I looked at Mariette's face. She searched for bad reasons, swearing that a woman's sensibility could not suit a man, and that her modesty could not suffer the slightest pinch—in brief, puerilities that caused me to realize the extent to which self-love is the prevalent sentiment even in the hearts of those nearest to us.

When he was alone with me again, Palestrino said: "Since you're going to court, obtain permission from the King to address yourself to some condemned criminal— someone bound for the galleys for instance. We can make two people happy at a stroke."

The idea appealed to me strongly, and I awaited the arrival of my coach impatiently. Instead of being shaken in the room with the moving walls, I remained fixed in one of its corners, still pressurized by the same sticky masses, and that relative repose spared me the nausea while leaving me the fever. All in all, my condition was bearable, and when the coach stopped in front of the door, at four o'clock in the afternoon, I climbed up the steps without too much trouble, sustained by Mariette, dressed up like a reliquary, in the midst of a crowd of ecstatic gossips.

The Chevalier was waiting for us in front of the palace. He took us through several gilded reception-rooms and introduced us into a final room in which a bejeweled

35

band of courtiers and courtesans[8] seemed to be awaiting our arrival.

Palestrino had accompanied us. He started commenting on me, pirouetting and offering excuses, speaking more nasally than ever. Lords and ladies touched me in a thousand ways, and I thought about the caprices of destiny. Who would have predicted, a week before, that I, a simple herbalist would be having my cheeks pinched and my calves pricked by the noblest fingers in the kingdom a week later?

Suddenly, everyone fell silent. The Queen came in. Malevolent drawings misrepresent her; public malignity has made her into a haughty foreigner. To me she seemed tall, with a fine figure, jovial and easy-going. She was staring at me when the King appeared. I had never seen him at such close range. He was wearing a blue suit. In spite of his large head and short legs, he was nothing less than majestic. While everyone bowed, he advanced toward me and addressed these words to me, which will be engraved in my heart for as long as I live: "Here's our man, then!"

An instant later, Palestrino launched into a long speech.

I had recognized Bailli in the audience, and was very glad that a more subtle scientist could describe my case appropriately. The agent of the Faculty raised a few objections, which the Italian refuted disdainfully.

The King seemed interested. The back of my hand had the supreme honor of being scratched by the

---

[8] The "editor" inserts a footnote here saying *sic*, meaning that Phlipot has committed the understandable error in his manuscript of thinking that a *courtisane* [courtesan] is a female *courtisan* [courtier] rather than an upmarket whore.

Queen's fingernails. Louis refused to touch me. He said a few words to the Chevalier, and was about to withdraw when I flung myself at his knees and cried in a plaintive voice: "Sire! I have a plea to address to you. I can't live like this any longer. Will His Majesty authorize me to take the sensibility of one of his galley-slaves?"

"They're the law's galley-slaves," the King replied, and I stopped short, blushing. He added: "That's Lenoir's business.[9] Bonsoir, Messieurs."

The Chevalier had stayed behind. "His Majesty," he told me, "has been generous enough to grant you a pension of 600 *livres*, from the Treasury." This news filled me with joy, even though I thought I had displeased the King. The Chevalier went on: "I'll obtain an audience with Lenoir—but why do you need a galley-slave? You'll find many a poor prisoner here in Paris who'll be only too happy to satisfy you for a little money."

And it was, therefore, thanks to the Chevalier that Palestrino and I were introduced to the presence of a certain Jean Ledoux, condemned to the scaffold after preliminary mutilation, for unspeakable crimes. Palestrino demonstrated to him that he would obtain a double advantage from the deal, given that I would pay 100 *écus* to his widow and that he would suffer no pain under torture.

Ledoux allowed himself to be convinced, and Palestrino commenced his passes, carrying out—according

---

[9] Jean-Charles-Pierre Lenoir (1732-1807) was Louis XVI's Lieutenant-General of Police in 1784, although he also had the job of looking after the King's library. In 1785, he was promoted to finance minister, but had no chance of coping with the nation's dire financial problems.

to his own terms—a double operation; first he charged a *mumie* with the sensibility of Ledoux; then, making me hold that *mumie*, he put me "in a state of rapport" with it, and caused all the fluid it contained to pass into me. After that, he took hold of me, and slapped me.

Two cries replied to his action: one from me, and one from Ledoux, whose sensibility had been incorporated into me. The criminal was suffocating with fear. We did not waste any time giving him further explanations. I limited myself to assuring him that he would only experience exquisite sensations.

Once outside the prison, as I was confirming my ability to feel by means of a series of proofs, Palestrino said: "It must be admitted that you don't have a very scientific mind. You haven't even asked me what has become of your former sensibility."

"Well," I replied, "I'm asking you now."

"It still binds your *mumie* to you, for your body is its substrate, and it has no faculties of its own. But it is prowling at the door, if I might put it thus, its place being occupied by the Ledoux's sensibility—you also being Ledoux's *mumie*. Do you understand?"

"Barely," I told him. "But I'm too happy for reasoning at present."

"Observe also," Palestrino said, "that your new sensibility will not adapt itself right away to your mental 'habitat.' It's up to you to fashion it."

He continued talking, but I was only thinking about going into a pastry-maker's shop in order to verify whether I had recovered the taste of good things. I observed its return with so much pleasure that I had to make an effort to stop myself embracing the shopkeeper. At first, I attributed that impulse to joy, but it was repeated very precisely in the presence of all women, even old ones.

I told Palestrino about this strange disturbance of my senses. "Don't forget," he told me, "that you have Ledoux's sensibility. You know what crime led him to the scaffold—but you are a *living* and intelligent *mumie*. Educate your sensibility, Phlipot."

I understood, and reproached him for having inserted the sensibility of a brute into me.

"Wasn't it you," he said, "who made me use the first Ledoux we found? My God, you were in a hurry! Anyway, I can take it out again."

I shut up, simultaneously happy and contrite. Palestrino had to restrain me several times as ladies went by. "Do you know," he said, when we were in my street, "that you're a very enviable person. There's the excellent Madame Phlipot. Give her my regards."

In fact, a few moments later, Mariette said to me tenderly: "That rest has done you good, my love! The adventure ought to be blessed!"

A sentiment of pride that men will understand prevented me from revealing to her that I had received another man's sensibility. I suffered in consequence, for a scandal burst out that same day, in spite of my best efforts, in my own home.

I was sitting quietly at the counter when I saw one of Mariette's friend come in: Madame Malotteau, an agreeable woman, the proprietress of a wash-house on the Seine, situated not far from the place where I had lost my *mumie*. Now, before I even had time to think, I seized the lady round the waist and kiss her full on the lips.

Mariette arrived in response to her screams and separated me from her with blows of her fists and fingernails. To calm her down, I told her what had happened in the prison. She did not believe a word of it, and continued to consider me guilty until the morning when the gazette had reported that a man named Jean Ledoux had been subjected to having his ears cut off while uttering cries of sensual delight. I had doubtless been in Mariette's arms, exercising his sensibility, at the exact moment of his torture.

My wife forgave me, but from that moment on, her jealousy knew no bounds. I was, therefore, harassed without respite and also lost my reputation, the chaste Madame Malotteau having taken care to tell anyone and everyone that I was afflicted with erotic delirium.

"It's no laughing matter," I said to Palestrino the following day. "I'd rather become permanently insensitive again than commit the crimes that led Ledoux to his ruin. I want a normal sensitivity, so that…"

I could not finish! I uttered a scream, feeling my former dolors revive: flattening against moving walls, inundation from head to toe.

Palestrino checked the time. "Fools that we are!" he said, striking his forehead. "They've just hung Ledoux; his sensibility has died with him, and yours, infusing your *mumie*, immediately insinuated its effluvia into you."

"How I'm suffering!" I replied. "So much mass is weighing upon my body that it's driving me into the wall. For pity's sake, save me from this torture!"

After mature reflection, we conceived the plan of putting up posters offering to buy a sensibility that was as good as new. I dared not expect potential sellers, but they came. I was visited by bailiff's men, physicians and speculators—but they all thought that they would be selling their moral sensibility. As soon as the realized that I was asking for their physical sensibility, they were out of the door at a run.

I increased my offers and made my requirements more precise. No old men, as I had expected. I saw rejected lovers, but I thought that if the cruel objects of their affection changed their minds, they would come to demand that I call off the deal. There were also misanthropes, but the merchandise, often of fine quality, lacked resistance. A usurer offered to lend me his, renewable at his discretion; I threw him out.

Finally, reflecting that there was a strong chance that any sensibility for sale would be afflicted by some hidden vice, and that even supposing that I acquired a good one, it would never be as good my own, fashioned since infancy to my body and mind, I had the posters torn down and abandoned myself to my catastrophic fate...

For two days my condition did not change at all, but at dawn on the third, my sufferings became keener than usual. The walls of my prison were tossing me around in all directions; heavy and flaccid weights were pressing down on my body and causing it to lose what equilibrium it had. Palestrino and Mariette were holding me up. Panting and suffocating, I was about to faint when the horrible pressure ceased and everything around me became calm. Already, I was able to breathe again. An instant afterwards, though, mad with pain, I howled: "Mercy! I'm being scalded! Ah! I'm boiling!" Then, overwhelmed by the pain: "Mariette! Palestrino, I'm dying!"

Just as my wife expected to see me die in her arms, however, there I was, with my eyes open, breathing deeply and weeping tears of joy, crying: "It's over! I'm no longer in pain! I'm in the open air! A gentle breeze is playing over me! But my God, what's happening? What's happening?"

Palestrino gnawed his fists. Mariette opened her mouth like a frog. And their surprise no longer knew any bounds when, stretching in my chair, I gave every sign of perfect sensual delight. "What's that! O sweetness! O delight!"

But the pleasant sensation faded away and I spent two days without experiencing any further pleasure or discomfort.

"May Heaven grant that I remain in this state," I said, "if it's written that I shall never see my *mumie* again."

At the end of the third day, though, I felt a stabbing sensation in my behind, and at the same instant, I cried out: "Something's sticking into me, I'm being transpierced! I'm being impaled, impaled!" Sweat was running off me in huge droplets.

"Perhaps he's among the infidels," said Mariette, terrified. "It's said that they impale Christians."

"No, Madame," said Palestrino, "but the absurdity of your hypothesis suggests to me a very plausible alternative." He turned to me. "It's impossible," he said, "that your *mumie* can have ended up very far from here—by which I mean more than 600 meters. You're experiencing the influence with too much precision and too much intensity. Now, an idea has just occurred to me." I admired the fertility of his genius yet again. "Posters and placards run a strong risk of escaping notice. As the *mumie* remains in the vicinity, I'll draft an advertisement, of which I'll have 5000 copies run off within four hours. With my printed sheets, I'll run to the

Dépôt Blanchard,[10] charter a Montgolfier, and strew a cloud of brochures from a height, describing the *mumie* and promising an honest reward to anyone who brings it to you."

With my hands on my behind, I agreed to everything. Mariette gave Palestrino an advance of five *louis*, and he disappeared.

I spent the time that followed in the midst of atrocious pains. It was, furthermore, impossible for me to sit down.

Now, in the afternoon of the same day, five or six hours after the Italian's departure, Madame Malotteau, the proprietress of the wash-house, whom I had provided with powerful excuses, came in quest of news of me. We sat her down in the back of the shop. Weeping all the while, I was telling her about my torture when the pupils of my eyes, which were fixed on the shawl that she was wearing, must have dilated in a truly terrifying fashion, for I saw her—along with Mariette—flatten herself against the wall, screaming in terror.

With one bound, however, I was upon her, and with a sweeping gesture I tore from the shawl a little cylinder as long as a thumb, of a pretty saffron color: my *mumie*, my dear *mumie*!

---

[10] Jean-Pierre Blanchard was an important pioneer of ballooning, who made his first successful ascent on March 2, 1784 in a hydrogen balloon, little more than three months after the first successful manned flight, by Pilâtre de Rozier and the Marquis d'Arlanders, in a hot air balloon constructed by the Montgolfier brothers (hence the description of balloons as "montgolfiers"). Blanchard had, however, decamped to London by August, and would not have been in Paris at this juncture of the story.

I saw a large pin stuck in the base of the cylinder. I threw it away. The impression of impalement disappeared immediately. I laughed; I wept; I stamped my feet with joy. Mariette joined in the chorus. Madame Malotteau sat there, stupidly.

Finally, in a voice punctuated with hiccups of joy, I said to her: "My *mumie*, my *mumie*! Bless you, you who impaled me, for I owe to that suffering the good fortune of having recovered my *mumie*!" Meanwhile, she darted anxious glances at the door.

Mariette reassured her. I sat down, without the slightest discomfort, and showed her the figurine. "It has within it," I said, "my sensibility, for which I have wept so much!"

"What? In that little doll? If I'd known, you would have had it sooner."

"What do you mean? Speak, quickly! Where did you find it?"

She hesitated, then came to a decision. "Bah! Between friends, that can be confided. Know that, from time to time, when the desire for duck soup overtakes us, we trap one of the river ducks in the pools. Three days ago, I was gutting one of them before putting it in the pot—and on slitting its gizzard, I saw a little shiny stem. At that moment, someone called me, and I threw it in the saucepan by mistake—but a minute later…"

"A century," I murmured.

"…having come back into the kitchen, I fished it out with a ladle, cleaned it carefully, and shut it in a drawer. I was no longer thinking about it when, opening the drawer by chance just now, I saw that it resembled a little doll, and I planted it on a pin that lacked a head. That's the whole story."

From the very first words I had sat there open-mouthed, as if to catch the idea that was floating before my eyes. Little by little, I had understood everything: that vice, the duck's beak...the narrow tube, its esophagus...the moving wall, the wall of its stomach, which must have retained me involuntarily, my *mumie* fortunately not being digestible.

Yes, a greedy duck had swallowed it, unseen[11] by Bailli's men, while they were turning over the mud. The evidence was dazzling.

Leaving Mariette the task of enlightening her friend, I placed my *mumie* delicately in my pocket, and ran like a streak of lightning to the Dépôt Blanchard.

"Chartering a Montgolfier," I said to myself, on the way, is not such a simple matter. "Blanchard can't have had more than two or three ready, and Palestrino probably hasn't taken off yet."

I was coming through the doors of the depot when I saw heads look up on all sides. The Italian rose up serenely, pouring cascades of printed sheets over the crowd. Perhaps he saw me, gesticulating like a lost soul and howling at him to come back down, but he must have mistaken my gestures and cries for signs of a cordial farewell, for he continued rising into the air...

I could do nothing more but wait.

I'll reimburse him, I said to myself, *for the expenses of the ascent*. That responsibility seemed trivial by comparison with my delight.

---

[11] The phrase I have translated as "unseen" is "*à l'invu*," an unorthodox formulation to which Falk attaches the footnote *sic*, calling attention to its similarity to "*à l'insu*" [unwittingly].

I had, therefore, set out on the return journey when I cry suddenly sprang up, uttered by all those who were following the progress of the machine. I hardly had time to raise my eyes; the Montgolfier, in flames and ripped apart, was falling to Earth—but well before then, the body of its unfortunate passenger crashed into the ground.

Everyone ran to him; he had been killed instantaneously.

Blanchard stopped the horses. "I only had a machine using the Pilâtre system available—but the gentleman affirmed that he was familiar with it!"[12]

As for me, moved to tears, I forced myself to assemble a group of good people, who were helping me to carry the dead man back to his room when I suddenly recalled, as swift and clear as a flash of lightning, a passage from the letter he had addressed to me: "Save for God, only the person..." But God was on high, and the poor fellow very far away!

Thus, at the very moment when I counted on seeing my martyrdom end, pitiless fate extended its term indefinitely. I went back home, plunged in bleak depression. I had already passed through so many alternations of hope and despair that as she listened to me narrating the catastrophe, Mariette discovered the pale smile of the fatalist upon my lips.

---

[12] The nature of the crash suggests that Palestrino was using a hydrogen balloon rather than a hot air balloon, but it is not obvious why this should be referred to as the "Pilâtre system;" it might be an ironic reference to the fact that Pilâtre de Rozier became one of the first people to die in an air-crash, along with his companion, during an attempt to cross the English Channel by balloon in June 1785.

"At least," she said, to console me, "if many pleasures are denied to you, in return, you will be spared all pain; it will be sufficient to place the *mumie* at the bottom of a drawer, on a nice feather cushion. And am I not here to caress it?"

And that was how I lived, detesting my *mumie* and cherishing it at the same time. Doubtless my infirmity would have rendered me melancholy at length, if Heaven had not soothed the bitterness with a subterfuge. Having become famous, in my fashion, I saw a procession of visitors file through my home, so I charged them an entrance fee. For a few *sous*, the vulgar were admitted to contemplate the *mumie*, lying beneath a glass globe. Before more qualified people, I carried out experiments. I composed an account of my ordeal, which Mariette recited from memory. There were gala sessions. We were able to move house, hire a lackey, and I amassed a tidy sum—to the extent that it was deemed in high places that my pension ought to be withdrawn: one more trick performed by Monsieur Calonne,[13] who only rewarded the artisans of his fortunes.

The operation was distasteful to me, but it did me no harm. People came to see me from all over Frances and abroad; several doctors attempted to substitute for Palestrino, but none was able to return my sensibility to me, and my case only became more admirable.

---

[13] Charles de Calonne (1734-1802) was appointed Controller-General of Finances on November 3, 1783, charged with the hopeless task of repairing the nation's finances; he immediately instituted a huge tax-raising plan that proved extremely unpopular with the relevant tax-payers, especially as Calonne was a notorious spendthrift. He was sacked in 1787 and exiled.

In the meantime, I read the philosophers, notably Locke and Condillac.[14] I refuted several of the former's views in an opuscule,[15] which I dedicated to the Marquise d'Armoise. I was featured in books, plays, and even parodies. I commend to the just scorn of the reader a wicked comic pageant entitled "Les Docteurs modernes," put on by Italian actors. The *Almanach des Muses* reviewed it, for which I can hardly be expected to congratulate it.[16]

Naturally, I made the acquaintance of authors, and men of the nobility, the sword and finance. One of them, a very pleasant fellow, got me into the grain business, where I tripled my fortune. Then he advised me as to a certain speculation whose success he guaranteed. I followed his advice and saw the shares rise joyfully. Then, one evening in November—I shall remember it forev-

---

[14] John Locke (1632-1704) was the founder of British empiricism, and a powerful influence on the French Encyclopedists. His notion of identity stood in frank contradiction to the ideas of the "magnetizers," and is incompatible with the substance of Phlipot's adventure. Etienne de Condillac (1715-1780) was one of Locke's most prominent French followers, and a close friend of the Encyclopedists.

[15] This diminutive of the Latin *opus* was once widely used to signify a small or minor work, but has fallen out of fashion.

[16] Falk inserts a footnote reference: "*Almanach des Muses de 1785*, page 323." The annual in question had been founded in 1762, with the innovative prospectus of publishing a selection of contemporary poetry in each issue as well as the usual almanac fare. Voltaire—Locke's first popularizer in France and a close friend of Condillac's—was its most frequent contributor; it was regarded as rather staid and conservative, although it printed the *Marseillaise* in 1793 and the Marquis de Sade's eulogy to Marat in 1794.

er—he came knocking at my door, in frightful weather, a late season storm more terrible than all those of the summer. "Your shares will drop very rapidly," he told me. "Sell them tomorrow. It's tomorrow that Necker's book on financial administration will appear, a few pages of which I have been able to read. The Genevois is malign—he's picking his moment to bring off a coup on the Bourse. Sell tomorrow."

I thanked my friend for having warned me, in spite of the tempest. A rapid calculation showed me that a fall, even a slight one, would take all my assets, and more besides. Already, I was in despair. "Bah!" he said. "The loss is nothing to you, who bear your fortune within yourself. Travel the world. In two months, you'll be richer than you were yesterday evening. Goodbye…I have other friends to warn."

He left. The storm was raging. In the intervals between claps of thunder, I discussed the future with Mariette. Henceforth, no more speculations…

As I completed these words, a bolt of lightning split the clouds, accompanied by a crash that deafened us; to my indescribable terror, a ball of fire emerged from the fireplace, crossed the room and vanished into the wall. At the same time, we were both bowled over by the electric shock.

Then there was a tumult throughout the house. Louison, who was with us, was the first to get up, unhurt. Mariette was completely nude; the lightning had reduced her clothing to dust. She had not suffered the slightest injury. As for me I had bumped my forehead on the corner of a table I got up bleeding, moaning with pain…with pain!

Sharp as it was, it immediately gave way to astonishment, and then to joy. Without paying any heed to the cries of "Fire!" resounding from the floor below, I bounded about, delirious with happiness, crying to Heaven: "It's back!" I would have thrown myself into the flames in order to feel them burn!

Meanwhile, down below, the cries became sparser; the nascent fire had been snuffed out. Mariette, reassured in that regard, was as utterly delighted as I was, and we fell to our knees, thanking Providence. Good old Palestrino! When he had written to me: "Save for God, only one person..." he had not known how truly he spoke! The man was dead, but God had realized the miracle!

In the judgment of the magnetizers, who provided a natural explanation afterwards, the lightning had passed through the casket that enclosed my *mumie*; the latter had remained intact but it had melted and liquefied, and my liberated sensibility had immediately reintegrated with my body. They took care to add that a similar result could not have be obtained simply by heating the *mumie*, because my sensibility would have been grilled with it, but that the lightning possessed magnetic virtues, still ill-defined, which separated the constituent fluids from bodies.[17]

At any rate, at the time, I was giving thanks whole-heartedly when Mariette started. "Unfortunates that we are," she cried, "we'll be irredeemably ruined!"

---

[17] The magnetizers of 1784 would have been familiar with the phenomenon of ball lightning, especially with the unwise experiment carried out in 1753 by Georg Richmann of Saint Petersburg, who attempted to replicate Benjamin Franklin's kite-flying experiment of the previous year but was killed by ball lightning that travelled down the string of his kite and struck him on the forehead. His clothes were singed, but he did not actually end up naked. It was Franklin who popularized the notion that lightning is due to a discharge of static electricity.

It was true. In the excess of my joy, I had forgotten my speculation. I remembered the saying that an unexpected joy can often be followed by catastrophe, and since that disagreeably memorable evening, at the end of my marvelous adventure, endowed with a wife who reproaches me every day for having ceased to be a prodigy, less sure of marrying Louison to a marquis than to an apothecary, I have returned to the herbalist's shop bearing the *Palm Oils* sign, as poor and sensible as before.

NOTE

Sébastien Phlipot's adventure may seem implausible to some readers. We shall refer them to two books which, among many others, are of indisputable scientific value, one entitled *L'Extériorisation de la sensibilité* by Colonel A. de Rochas, former administrator of the Ecole Polytechnique (Paris: Chamuel 1895) and the other *Le Magnétisme Vital* by M. Ed. Gasc-Defossés, a member of the Institut Général Psychologique, prefaced by M. E. Boirac (Paris: Rudeval 1907).[18]

The hypothesis of magnetic fluid acting on living beings and matter has now been scientifically demonstrated—cf. the galvanometer of M. de Puyfontaine, *Le Magnétisme Vital*.[19]

MM. Boirac and de Rochas have often carried out Palestrino's procedure. After clearly distinguishing his

---

[18] Lieutenant-Colonel Albert de Rochas d'Aiglun (1837-1914) became a prolific writer on various "paranormal" topics following his retirement from military service. The references to the cited book are genuine, and the other text cited here also exists, although it is now extremely rare (the Bibliothèque Nationale does not have a copy). The contributor of the preface to the latter volume, Emile Boirac (1851-1917), became much better known than the book's author, though more for his promotion of Esperanto than his psychic research.

[19] The Baron de Puyfontaine's claim to be able to influence the movement of a galvanometer needle by the power of his mind is cited in numerous books on parapsychology, all copying from one another, but the source of the anecdote remains unclear.

experiment from the puerile practices of spell-casting, M. de Rochas expresses himself thus on p.101:

"After observing that the wax to be modeled is one of the substances appropriate to store the sensibility of the majority of exteriorized subjects, I fashioned a statuette with the wax and placed it upright in front of one of the subjects in order to flood it, and I ascertained that if I pricked the statuette's head, the subject experienced discomfort in the upper part of the body; he experienced it in the lower part if I pricked the statuette beneath its feet...

"I succeeded in localizing the sensibility by cutting a lock of hair from the nape of the subject's neck while asleep and implanting it in the head of the statuette. When the subject was woken up, he was unaware of the operation to which I had just subjected him; I placed myself out of his sight and I pulled the hairs embedded in the wax. The subject immediately turned round, saying: 'Who pulled my hair?'

"In general, the sensation is only transmitted over a distance of five or six meters; one day, however, the subject, Madame Vix, had terminated a session in which I had experimented with a wax figure; she returned home and I was following her with my eyes as she went through a large courtyard when M. B., who was with me, had the idea of pricking the wax; I immediately saw Madame Vix lean down and rub her leg."

Now, nothing hinders the supposition that Palestrino was an exceptionally-endowed individual, the possessor of an intense magnetic power, capable of flooding a *mumie* powerfully enough for the subject to remain in rapport with it and distances far greater than five or six meters; there would only be a difference of degree, and not of nature, between that operation and those that are executed today.

On the question of whether a subject can be exteriorized in a waking state as well as during his sleep, cf. the experiment of April 26, 1893 "on Madame O., who exteriorizes very easily even in a awaking state" (*Extériorisation de la sensibilité*, p.107), the experiments of June 27, 1892 (p.222), December 1893 (p.232) and November 1892 (by M. Demarest, p.238); and cf. M. Boirac's experiment on a woken subject (*Magnétisme animal*, p.264)

On the question of whether the *mumie* gradually allows the fluid stored within it to escape, nothing hinders the supposition that Palestrino had composed an amalgam retained sensibility for a much longer period than those presently known. Again, a difference or more or less, of degree and not of nature.

THE MASTER OF THE THREE STATES

When I recall this fantastic history, sprawling in a real armchair and smoking a veritable cigar, it seems like a dream. Nevertheless, it happened—and I found myself mixed up in it at a critical time in my life. And it was me who put an end to its vicissitudes, by virtue of a terrible irresponsibility for which I still feel remorse. I am, however, counting on the final confession that my story will comprise to liberate my conscience completely. Perhaps certain aspects of my actions will allow me to be more than absolved: that is for my sovereign judge, the reader, to decide.

I. Two Disconcerting Phenomena

My name is Mesmin Cabri. I am 26 years old. In 1910, my parents, notable tradespeople who lived in a provincial town, sent me to study law in Paris. My mind did, indeed, possess juridical abilities, and I nurture the hope of succeeding my patron, the advocate Maître X*** in his responsibilities. Having been taken into his chambers in the position of clerk in 1911, I quickly attracted his attention, with the result that, in July 1913, at which time I obtained my qualification, he raised my monthly wage by 3.50 francs.

My physique is agreeable; I have an abundance of light chestnut-colored hair, a rosy complexion, a blond moustache, even white teeth and nicely-spaced green eyes. Symmetrical in my medium build, I know how to wear clothes and sustain a conversation. My faults—for I am being frank—are a slight overfondness for good food and feet that are perhaps a trifle large; my good qualities are intelligence, generosity, a good memory and modesty. That is enough of an introduction, since my role in this story will be entirely in the background.

Well-equipped, all things considered, with a clerk who did him honor, my employer did not neglect to invite me to receptions frequented by the society of the Court and High Finance. One evening, he even took me to an almost-intimate dinner, since I only counted, apart from myself, a dozen guests, who made me welcome when I arrived.

Now, in the course of one soirée at his home, I met an adorable creature, Suzanne Bic, the daughter of

Maître Bic, a bailiff. We chatted, we danced, each charmed by the other. Rivals emerged in the meantime—who, indeed, would not have been smitten at first glance with that exquisite redhead with the fine figure, an apricot complexion, mouse-grey eyes, symmetrical teeth, arranged between her lips like fresh almonds in a divided strawberry?—but I seduced her right away, and that is a fact. We discovered that we had the same tastes: in literature, heroic drama; in music, Italian opera; in cakes, rum baba; in architecture, Louis XV style. In brief, to complete the ecstasy, we promised ourselves to one another.

I knew how to ingratiate myself with Maître Bic, a corpulent and ruddy-faced but worthy individual with short-cropped hair and a gold-rimmed pince-nez, by talking to him about unpaid debts and forced sales, and with the tall and dark Madame Bic, by escorting her to the buffet seven times. Recommended to them by my patron as a young man full of promise, they authorized me to pay them a visit in their fifth-floor apartment in the Rue Dante—a permission of which I took advantage the following Sunday. Need I go on? Monsieur Bic resigned himself, saw my parents, and came back satisfied. A month later, Suzanne and I, shivering with excitement, exchanged the chaste rings of betrothal.

A future of blue skies! I dazzled my future family with my knowledge, my manners and my wit. I loved to sustain, not without a certain brio, original opinions that alarmed the Bics, especially Madame, who was credulous and limited; I experienced the delicate pleasure of simultaneously amusing and troubling my tender Suzanne, emotional angel that she was. At the pronunciation of a paradox, she would say to me, blushing: "You frighten me, Mesmin!" Her bosom palpitated, she breathed lightly, and I collected the kiss suspended from her lips.

Everything was smiling upon me, then—even the household dog, a little fox-terrier name Fredaine, which Suzanne adored and which I stuffed with sugar candy. I had not the slightest inkling of the setbacks that were lying in wait for our happy plans.

One evening, Bic said to me: "Mesmin, an ambition that my wife and I have been nurturing is about to be fulfilled. We're beginning to get old and are having difficulty climbing stairs. Now, I've been able to rent a little house in Auteuil at a very affordable price, to which we are moving right away. I'm losing a month's rent, but I want to take advantage of the opportunity."

Although the news was of scant importance to me, I congratulated Bic warmly. My tender Suzanne went on: "Since you're about to spend three weeks with your parents, you'll find us in residence when you return."

"And you can help us choose the wallpaper, as you're a man of taste," her mother added.

I replied wittily, and as I was leaving Paris that evening, I obtained official permission to kiss my fiancée on the cheeks—an operation that, it goes without saying, had been effected many times unofficially. I shook Bic's hand, kissed Madame's, stroked Fredaine and left.

How my heart was beating three weeks later, as I emerged from the Metro that had brought me from the Avenue des Ternes, where I lived, to Auteuil station! On descending from the train I had a quick snack, tidied myself up a little, bought a bouquet of white roses and hastened toward the new residence of Suzanne and her parents. Eight o'clock was chiming. Nightfall, already imminent, was attenuating the heat of an August day.

The Rue La Fontaine was long. I finally drew near to my paradise, and even recognized it at a distance, from the memory of a drawing that Suzanne had made me of its silhouette.

Finally, here I am! The entrance door is open. I go in, surprised not to encounter anyone, passing into a dark and sinuous corridor. Suddenly, a voice becomes audible at the far end of the corridor, shrill and fearful. I can't tell whether it's the voice of a man or a woman.

"Who's there? Who's there? Close the door, Eusèbe!"

I understand that I've got the wrong house. I turn around hurriedly, without making any reply, and once outside I look at the house number by the light of the risen Moon: 68, instead of 98! To the Devil with these little houses that all look alike!

In the street, I hasten toward my true objective—but as I walk, I experience a bizarre visual sensation: I seem to see, flying through the clear night, vague large forms of birds, and bounding across the street the giant and vaporous apparitions of various animals!

I attributed this hallucination of sorts to the hyper-sensitivity of my nervous system, focused on my fiancée, and finally rang the bell at number 98, where the round face of the chambermaid, Sophie, who came to open to door to me, caused me to utter a faint cry of re-lived satisfaction.

"I'm really here this time!" I exclaimed, gaily. "Monsieur, Madame and Mademoiselle Bic are at home I hope?"

"Yes, Monsieur Cabri," Sophie replied, introducing me into the drawing-room.

My Suzanne and her parents gave me a friendly welcome, but as if they were inhibited by some anxiety.

Caught up in the joy of seeing them again, I did not take account of it at first, and politely waxed lyrical about the beauty of the little house and the charm of the drawing-room, whose large bay window opened via a few steps into a garden. The warm night was perfumed; Suzanne seemed to me more delightful than ever. Sitting next to her, however, beneath a lamp, I saw that her beautiful eyes had been weeping.

"What grief has clouded your eyes?" I asked.

She sighed.

Madame Bic replied on her behalf. "You know Fredaine, our pretty little fox-terrier?"

"What about him?"

Suzanne went on, in tears: "Lost! Lost since yesterday! I love animals so much! Poor little dear!" And she burst into sobs.

I consoled her as best I could, somewhat vexed to discover that my presence did not compensate for the absence of an animal.

Maître Bic, however, declared: "You might well cry. You're being punished for your negligence."

"Negligence!" Suzanne protested. "Oh, Papa! He must have got out and got lost in an area that's new to him."

"Got lost! What about his sense of smell! He's been stolen," opined Madame Bic.

The discussion resumed, heatedly, even bitterly—and as Fredaine continued to play the principal role, while I and my bouquet of roses remained confine to subaltern parts, I assumed an air of cool dignity, which did not seem to be to Suzanne's taste, for she criticized me thus: "Oh, I know very well that you detested him!"

"Me, Suzanne!"

"Yes, you. You played practical jokes on him—you pinched his tail and struck his nose as if to kill him!"

"Oh!"

She moved away from me to a settee, to sulk in the shadows beside the pen bay-window. Her parents started a game of piquet under the lamp. Naturally, I went to join Suzanne and knelt at her feet. How divine she was in that half-light! I murmured passionate protests to her in a warm, low voice. She turned her head toward the wall, but her hand was already linked with mine. Weary of kneeling, I gradually raised myself up, in order to sit on a little footstool set next to the settee.

As I sat down, however, a disconcerting phenomenon was manifest beneath me; instead of feeling, on contact, a hard and shiny wooden surface, I seemed to penetrate a gelatinous mass. At the same time my posterior exhaled a kind of confused moan—a muffled plaint like the hoot of a distant owl.

I bounded to me feet, and I saw...

I saw the dog Fredaine, in person, but in an appearance such that I was left speechless, and Suzanne sat there open-mouthed, in a petrified pose.

Her fox terrier was stretched on his belly along the footstool where I had just at down, but, while conserving his color and his fur, seemed no longer to have any but a doughy consistency. His paws—veritable feet of marshmallow, if I might put it thus—were dangling from the footstool on to the carpet; from his head, which he did not have the strength to hold up, to the end of his docked tail, which hung down like a stout piece of vermicelli, he was stretched out lamentably.

In brief, the dog was utterly soft, with the most disastrous, as well as the most unexpected, effect. In addition, he was emitting that kind of plaintive ululation that

I had believed, momentarily, to have issued from myself. For that semi-formless dog was alive—inexplicably alive!

Suddenly, the air was rent by piercing screams. Suzanne, prey to—or not far away from—a nervous crisis, was struggling in my arms, accusing me of being responsible: "My darling Fredaine! You've crushed him! You've sat on top of him, you wicked man!"

"Me, Suzanne!"

The Bics hurried over, looking at the abnormal fox-terrier with bleak bewilderment. I protested that, to all evidence, I had sat on the dog, but that, after all, I did not weigh enough to turn him, by virtue of that fact, into a mollusk; that if I had crushed the dog, he would have barked immediately on feeling me weigh upon him; and that, finally, I had had the impression of compressing a soft body rather than a solid one. These peremptory explanations were nevertheless unsuccessful; the family Bic, frozen in amazement, watched the animal get down, effortfully, from the footstool. Now he was crawling over the carpet, a sort of hairy cynocephalous jellyfish with the feet of an octopus. The vile beast!—but simultaneously so ridiculous, with his swaying muzzle, that in spite of the ambient mystery, I could not help smiling. It was a bad move.

"Look at him laughing, now!" cried Suzanne. "Making fun of the harm he's done!"

"You're abusing our hospitality, young man!" said Monsieur Bic, dryly.

"But Monsieur," I went on, impatiently, "must I demonstrate to you once again the innocence of my backside? A crushed dog, damn it, has never taken it into its head to live in a state of softness!"

"You're right," said Bic. "That is a surprising phenomenon…"

"Supernatural!" murmured Madame.

"Unless," her husband continued, looking at me severely, "it's one of those tricks that young clerks are accustomed to play. The clerks of the court have been known…"

"But, good God…!" I exclaimed, angrily.

I was not crying out too soon; a second, even more disconcerting, phenomenon had just become manifest. On the Bics' card-table, harshly lit by the lamp, a handsome white rabbit had just appeared—by what magic? It was pricking up its ears, very much alive!

"A rabbit!"

The same exclamation—imposed by the evidence of the fact—sprang from our lips, but our eyes, this time, were no longer projecting the same gaze. If mine only manifested surprise, those of the spouses Bic allied to astonishment a strong suspicion in my regard. In less than ten minutes, since my arrival, the family dog had been transformed into a kind of living pâté, and a rabbit, unseen until now, had established itself on a table, emerging from nowhere.

Monsieur Bic coughed, paused momentarily, and solemnly pronounced: "This new apparition has confirmed my suspicions. Monsieur Mesmin Cabri, would you be so good as to admit that we consider you to be some kind of trickster, a practical joker, without any regard for the young woman that you claim to love, and devoid of any respect for her parents. I have, in consequence, the honor of asking you to leave."

"But Monsieur Bic….!"

"Leave!" he repeated, inflexibly, his forefinger extended toward the door.

"Suzanne!"

This supplication awoke no echo. My fiancée, terrified, remained huddled against her mother, whose protective arms were wrapped around her.

"Oh, the horrid thing is leaving droppings on my card-table!"

In response to his wife's exclamation, Bic seized the rabbit by the ears,

"And take away your rodent!" he proffered, throwing it at my head.

I caught the symbolic animal in mid-air, and left, swearing to set to work immediately to recover the good graces of the angry parents and my bewildered fiancée.

II. The Outstretched Hand

Once outside, I wanted to persuade myself that I had been the victim of a dream, but the enigmatic rabbit attested the reality. I let the embarrassing herbivore drop on to the pavement; it fled in fear—and while heading toward the Metro, I thought hard. Should I go to the police? To some private detective? Would it not be better, in view of my intelligence, of which I was justly proud, to use my own perspicacity to solve the mystery?

One immediate difficult stopped me, however; the seat of the mystery was the Bic's house—"Castel Bic," according to the rather pretentious inscription decorating the threshold—and I had been expelled from Castel Bic. My self-respect prevented me from reappearing there in any other guise than a victorious Oedipus. Moreover, the rabbit impressed me less than the dog. The idea of an elastic fox-terrier persisted in confounding me, and I imagined with compassion the family's prolonged state of amazement in confrontation with that spectacle.

The memory of the nebulous forms that I had seen flying and bounding in the street further augmented my confusion. Had I really been the victim of an illusion? Involuntarily, I associated the incident with those at Castel Bic, without any plausible reason.

I got back to my room, therefore in an anxious perplexity, and I spent a restless night, sailed by dreams. I saw Monsieur Bic as a rich man, in the place of his respectable superior, with a ridiculous rabbit's head; mounted on a steam-roller, he crushed my tender Suzanne on the road before me; I found no more than a flattened fiancée, like a pancake, while her mother reproached me vehemently for climbing on to her card table.

In brief, after a series of discomfiting little naps, I got up in some distress, my mind painfully extended toward the Inexplicable, of which I was the victim. My Sunday being free, I headed for Auteuil as soon as I had drunk my milky coffee and my three croissants, as if propelled by a force.

As I emerged on to the Rue La Fontaine, I perceived groups of residents engaged in discussions outside the doors. In one compact assembly, I even distinguished a policeman. I drew nearer. He was writing down statements in a greasy notebook, whose tenor appeared to me to have a direct link with the previous evening's events. Several inhabitants of the quarter had seen the unexpected emergence, either in the open air or in their homes, of a cat, a guinea-pig or a rabbit. Some had seen birds. One had even seen a marmoset. As soon as it appeared, each of these animals, fully alive, had commenced the leaps, flutters or capers characteristic of its species.

The majority of the old crones were crying witchcraft. Silently, and with concentration, I lost myself in thought. Suddenly, an idea lit up in my brain, and I asked several people the following question, full of consequence in my judgment: "Was the window of the room in which the animal appeared open or closed?"

All of my interlocutors replied: "It was open."

From that reply I concluded, privately—with a swiftness of induction to which it pleases me to render homage—that these animals had come from outside.

I acquired, moreover, the certainty that all the apparitions had been produced between 9 and 10 p.m. the previous evening—consequently, at the same time as that of the Bic rabbit. They must, therefore, all have proceeded from an identical point of origin.

From then on, the whole of my perspicacity was devoted to the problem of finding the departure point of the invisible animals that became visible at the point of arrival. I am too intelligent to believe in the supernatural, and I persuaded myself, in consequence, that the problem must have a humanly acceptable solution. Although I spent the rest of the day in mediation and observation, in the street, the woods and in cafés, however, the formidable contention of my mind only ended up giving me a terrible headache.

I dined in the open air and took my drink neat, in a tavern in Auteuil, which attenuated my headache slightly. When dark fell, before going home, I wanted to see the Castle of Lost Love again as the sad Pedestrian Errant. For 20 minutes I stood, sighing, beneath the windows of Castel Bic; then, dragging myself away with some difficulty, I continued on my way. It was then— about 100 meters further on—that a new apparition exacerbated my bewildered faculties to the extreme.

The street was almost deserted; the walls extended whitely, bathed in moonlight. As I passed in front of a house I saw hand emerging from a partly-open window at the level of a low entresol, which flattened itself against the exterior wall: a hand that was normal size to begin with but which soon stretched out, becoming elongated, as if constituted of a fluid material, until it was nearly a meter long. Then a wrist and forearm appeared, creeping down the wall like a serpent.

I stood there stupefied, my eyes glued to the Mystery. Then, slowly, the wrist withdrew; the hand, doubtless having arrived at the limit of its elongation, came back up the wall, and the fingers, like five immense slugs, disappeared through the gap in the window, shrinking as they went.

I looked at the house more attentively, and, by an effort of memory, recognized it. It was the one into which I had gone by mistake the night before!

Impelled by curiosity, and even more so by a presentiment, careless of the dangers suspended over my head, I headed swiftly for the entrance door, hoping to find it open once again. It was closed. I rang repeatedly: no response. I hesitated for some time as to whether I ought to alert the police, but my legal knowledge reminded me that the law prohibits the violation of the homes of citizens after sunset. In any case, I preferred to have the sole honor of solving the prodigious enigma. Weary of ringing the doorbell, I drew away, resolving nevertheless to find out, without delay, what was going on in the house.

The street, as I have said, was almost deserted. There were only a few porters sitting in front of their lodges smoking their pipes, at widely-spaced intervals—which reminded me of the beautiful verses of the poet: "As soon as the heat becomes a little strong/All the concierges are on their doorsteps." The cheerful plumpness of one of them seemed to me to be heavy with confidences. I accosted him with an ingenious remark about the propitiousness of the warm weather for growing vegetables, and collected the following details:

The tenant of the house in question was a Monsieur Pitoulet, a widower with a private income. He lived alone, rarely went out and had few visitors. A daily woman came in to do his housework and cooking. He must be occupied with "electrical matters" because he had been seen taking various machines and instruments into the house, but he was secretive about his work; no

69

one, save for a young assistant, was allowed to go into a large building situated in the garden, whose key he kept on his person. The housekeeper was bad-tempered, but the assistant seemed communicative; many things might be found out from him, but he had disappeared the night before. At any rate, Monsieur Pitoulet was polite to everyone and paid his bills on time; he seemed rather eccentric.

I learned nothing more. I understood, however, why my repeated ringing had been in vain: Monsieur Pitoulet, alone by night, had been afraid to open his door. All in all, I could do no more than wait until the following day to resume my investigation. Convinced that I was on the right track, I went home content.

The following morning I asked in chambers for a day's leave in order to attend to urgent business. I reached Auteuil at 8:30 a.m., determined to shed some light, if not on other enigmas, at least on—if I might employ the style of popular fiction—"the mystery of the elastic hand."

III. Monsieur Pitoulet

I took care to ring the doorbell with polite discretion. I heard brief and muffled footsteps approaching. The sullen face of an old woman appeared at a little peep-hole.

"What do you want?" she demanded, peevishly.

I raised my straw boater and asked, politely: "Is Monsieur Pitoulet at home, Madame?"

"First, who are you?"

"I am Monsieur Mesmin Cabri—here's my card."

"Is Monsieur Pitoulet expecting you?"

"Yes," I replied.

"I'll go see."

She shut the peep-hole in my face. A few curious neighbors were watching me. I whistled, idly. The footsteps returned; the peep-hole reopened; the old women reappeared.

"Monsieur Pitoulet doesn't know you."

"Is that possible?"

"Get lost."

"I beg your pardon!" As usual, a fortunate inspiration occurred to me. "Would you please tell Monsieur Picoulet that I've come about *the elastic hand*."

"The elastic hand?"

"The very same. Go tell him. You'll find that he'll see me."

A further wait—but this time, the door opened. "Follow me," said the old woman, in a milder tone.

We went along the sinuous corridor and she introduced me into a brightly-lit room furnished as a study. I had scarcely entered when I saw a short, pale and thin man appear from a neighboring room. He seemed well-to-do, with a suspicion of a paunch. He was wearing a dressing-gown and a skull-cap with a tassel. His grey hair, rather long and combed back, uncovered a large forehead with bushy eyebrows, beneath which shone keen little black eyes. Above a salt-and-pepper moustache with waxed points was a narrow ruddy nose, and his chin was hidden by a pointed beard. In brief, it was the head of a shriveled and old-fashioned musketeer.

I bowed profoundly. He replied courteously, raising his skull-cap, and, holding my card in the tips of his fingers in an anxious manner, said in a shrill voice: "You want to see me, Monsieur? What about?"

I understood immediately that it was necessary not to treat the little man brusquely, and I replied mildly: "I permitted myself to disturb you, Monsieur, in the hope of rendering you a service. Yesterday evening, in front of your house, I perceived a hand emerging from a window that I can point out to you: a strange hand…"

I paused. He frowned, but remained silent.

I went on: "The hand was a living hand, which stretched inordinately…"

Another pause on my part. He swallowed his saliva, leaned on the back of a chair, and declared, with forced emphasis: "I confess, Monsieur, that I don't see why this story should interest me."

I then understood immediately that it would be better to treat the little man brusquely, and I replied forcefully: "Perhaps it will interest you when you know that I associate it with the disconcerting phenomena that I witnessed the evening before yesterday in this very street."

I watched his nose pass from red to cream. In a tremulous voice, which he tried to render ironic, he said: "Are you, by chance, a policeman?"

I seized the argument that was offered, and in a fit of eloquence, said: "Me! A policeman! Can you believe that, Monsieur? I am an honest young man who comes to you with a pure heart. I will tell you everything, Monsieur, laying my soul bare, for a presentiment whispers to me that you can save my compromised happiness. I am the fiancé of the most ideal of creatures, Mademoiselle Suzanne Bic, the daughter of Maître Bic, the well-known bailiff, who lives further along your street. She has banished me from her sight for having allegedly flattened her fox-terrier and caused the appearance of a rabbit that I had never seen before. Since then, I have tried in vain to vindicate myself. Now, I have learned that you are a great scientist as well as a worthy man. You can undoubtedly furnish me with a few scientific explanations of the surprising phenomena that I have reported to you, which will return my love to me. Oh, Monsieur, save my life!"

And I threw myself at his knees.

I heard him murmur: "The fox-terrier! Ah! The fox-terrier! That's it!" And he added, in a compassionate tone: "You poor young man. Get up, and we'll talk."

It was him who interrogated me—in a rather skillful fashion, I must say—with cross-checks designed to prove my frankness. I felt that I had gained his confidence.

Satisfied, he exclaimed: "I, Pitoulet, who have devoted myself to the happiness of humankind, do not want to be the cause of your unhappiness. Depend on me, young Cabri; I will give you back your fiancée."

"You are a good man, Monsieur Pitoulet!" And I threw my arms around him. We embraced momentarily.

Suddenly, he shouted: "Gudule!"

The daily woman appeared. "Make lunch for two," he ordered. Then he turned to me. "I'm inviting you. Since destiny seems to have desired to bring us together, I also have plans for you. I am, at this moment, conducting certain experiments, for which I require a devoted and discreet assistant. Will you be that assistant?"

"But am I qualified? Little versed in the sciences…"

"That's exactly what I need: relative ignorance; absolute devotion."

"But my job…I'm an advocate's clerk…"

"You'll leave your chambers. Suzanne is worth more than that," he concluded, slyly.

How was I able to explain to my patron, without difficulty, that family affairs demanded that I ask for extended leave? How was I able to obtain that leave immediately? Either I must have been persuasive, or he had no pressing need of my services at that moment. Whatever the reason, I returned to the Rue La Fontaine liberated.

During my absence—I have no idea how—Pitoulet must have verified the story of my engagement, for he welcomed me as if I were his own son, and we sat down to lunch cheerfully. He drank his wine neat, like me, and we imparted further confidences. In brief, after dessert, finding himself in perfect sympathy with his guest, he waited until Gudule had placed the coffee, cigars and liqueurs on the table, and then, not without solemnity, he expressed himself in these terms:

"First, I must ask for your word of honor not to reveal anything about the spectacle that you will shortly witness."

I swore a solemn oath. He continued:

"Cabri, chance favored you initially, by showing you that hand stretching along the wall; afterwards, it was a perfectly correct—and childishly simple—association of ideas that led you to think that I was no stranger to the phenomena in question, but before I explain them to you, permit me to tell you something about myself.

"I confided to you, between the Port-Salut and the apricots, that I had an unhappy marriage. To be more precise, my wife deceived me prodigiously. I had married the exuberant daughter of a large wallpaper manufacturer. Obliged to earn my own living from an early age, I had entered into his business as a mere employee. However, having an inventive mind with a scientific bent, I discovered a method of coloring that earned him a great deal of money.

"As I was working on a new invention, he offered me his daughter in order to attach me to him. I accepted, and I had reason, as is often the case, to congratulate myself on that decision, and also to regret it in certain respects—to regret it because, after two months of marriage, my wife attached herself to a series of lovers, successive or simultaneous, to the exclusion of myself; to congratulate myself on it because, henceforth sheltered from need, I was able to continue my research. I abandoned, of course, anything to do with wallpaper—which exasperated my father-in-law.

"I was already deemed to be an eccentric; I was soon charge with insanity, especially when certain papers that I had presented to the Académie proved incapable of attracting the attention of my official colleagues. I was nothing in their eyes but an irregular, a guerrilla of science, poorly regarded in the regular army of black and green cocked hats. Then again, I was devoid of urbanity, and had such a luminous nose…

"To cut a long story short, I complained to my father-in-law one evening about his daughter's misconduct—I had not dared to tackle my wife about it; she would have beaten me—and he submerged me in a cascade of insults, accusing me of having 'put one over on him.' He offered me by way of final settlement an income, on condition that I let the divorce go through on the grounds of my own faults and injuries. I accepted, for the sake of science but, being practical for once in my life, demanded a capital sum instead of a pension. To my father-in-law's dictation I wrote a few peremptory missives to imaginary ladies, was condemned by the court and, without delay, dedicated the price of my liberty to the installation of a laboratory.

"Having no needs, save for an occasional glass of good wine; all my small income was devoted to my studies. I have undertaken research of a special nature. It has lasted ten years, young man—but patience is the true form of scientific enthusiasm. This research has just reached a conclusion. You shall know what it was, and what its result has been."

Monsieur Pitoulet had risen to his feet, with his forefinger in the air, as if inspired—and he said: "Follow me!"

IV. The Great Transmutator

We left the room and went through the garden. In an open space behind a few tall trees, I discovered a sort of closed hangar, the door of which Pitoulet opened for me. I went into what seemed to be a vast machine-room. There were no windows, but the glazed roof let light in. There was a profusion of electric lamps hanging from wires or fixed to the walls. Insulated electrical cables ran along the white-enameled walls.

Almost in the center of the rectangular room, on a glass-paved platform, protected by a glass ramp, stood a black mass at least four meters high: a sort of giant cylinder, enveloped, so far as I could judge, with some sort of tarry coating. We made a tour of the room in which the black cylinder lay, turning left at the entrance door. The entire length of the left-hand wall was fitted with a little walkway, reached by means of three steps. On an immense white marble console bolted to the wall above the walkway at head-height, an array of switches and levers displayed a copper gleam. Pairs of thick black cables emerged from the console, criss-crossing above our heads like an enormous spider's web and disappearing into the central mass.

We headed for the back of the room, and I saw that the enormous cylinder terminated, at that end, in a shining cone that seemed to me to be made of copper. The braids of rings that encircled the cylinder in places similarly seemed to be copper. In front of the cone was an immense stool—or, more accurately, a platform—at least two meters square, composed of some black shiny material reminiscent of black lead. To the right of the platform, vertically placed at head height, a marble console analogous to the one fixed to the wall, but much smaller, supported a varied set of switches. Behind the black platform stood another strange apparatus, a kind of metallic grille, four meters high if not more, similar in form to a car radiator, maintained by brackets sunk into the floor.

We went around the grille, which was parallel to the wall, and came back toward the entrance on the other side of the room, where I noticed various objects, most notably an enormous glass bell-jar—destined for what nightmarish cheese?—a machine that seemed to me to be a rotatory pump, and a little cabin bearing the inscription: *Cloakroom*.

"That concludes the proprietor's tour," said Pitoulet, with a satisfied expression.

I made no reply, prey to a vertigo of utter incomprehension. I discerned, obviously, that it was an electrical installation of a special kind—but what? What was its purpose?

"You seem somewhat at a loss," Pitoulet remarked.

"Indeed!"

"Have you studied electricity?"

"Yes, at school."

"Poor boy! But it's a marvel, of a sort, since you don't understand it very well. I'll tell you enough to put you in the picture—the essential facts."

He went on:

"Know, therefore, Cabri, my friend, that one science has always been my passion: chemistry, the science of sciences, in sum; that which penetrates the depths of things in order to discover the principle, the essence. It is to all the natural sciences what metaphysics is to philosophy, with the difference, nevertheless, that metaphysics plays with dreams, while chemistry works upon the real. Ah! To decompose to the extremity of unity the bodies that compose nature, to finally discover the essential matter! But we are far from that goal, and who knows whether we shall ever achieve it? The essential matter draws away when one gets close to it, vanishes when one thinks one has grasped it, and there remains of it, in the ultimate analysis, no more than a word: Energy, imagined by scientists to lull their ignorance—a word that, you might well think, is not the proclamation of a victory but the confession of a defeat.

"Which will triumph in the end—man, who pursues, or nature, which hides? Man, I firmly believe, for man is nothing but conscious nature, determined to know itself. For my part, I have pushed my research into the constitution of matter as far as I can, but chemistry is an immense domain, one sole branch of which suffices for a man's career. I therefore devoted myself to the chemistry of organic bodies—but that branch still being too vast, I took one of its side-roads and devoted myself to biochemistry, the chemistry of living bodies. The constitution of living matter then became the object of my research.

"I resolved to begin, methodically, by studying the molecular structure of its component parts, and as the best means of getting to know the intimate structure of a body is the comparative study of its variant states, the ides occurred to me of submitting bodies to an influence capable of modifying them physically. It seemed to me that the influence in question might be obtained by means of an electrical force or, more precisely, that of a very powerful magnetic field. 'Very powerful' is an understatement; I resolved to create a magnetic field of unprecedented power and, not without difficulty and expense, I ordered the construction of the apparatus you see here, which is, as you have doubtless guessed…"

"No."

"Well, you're as ignorant as one could wish. Which is…an electromagnet."

"That enormous cylindrical mass?"

"Yes. That mass, covered with an insulating envelope, is simply the most powerful electromagnet in the world. I had it constructed in Pittsburgh, U.S.A. The wire coils contained in its spools contain several hundred tons of copper. By means of a process that I have discovered, which constitutes the greatest originality of the apparatus, no heating is produced in the metal, in spite of the immense quantity of electrical energy circulating within it. The recording devices installed at intervals testify to that absence of heat. I confess, however, that my cooling system necessitates the employment of liquid air. That large platform placed on insulators is made of graphite. It is set at the dead center of the magnetic field produced by the electromagnet. Finally, the enormous grille that you see standing behind it is linked to a series of metal pieces buried in the floor, in such a way that communication with the ground is perfect. Contrary to what might seem to be the case, the grille is not made of iron but of lead, a non-magnetic metal. It concentrates and reinforces the electromagnet's field of action, by limiting it.

"Once I was ready to bring this torrential source of magnetic energy into play, I began by studying the molecular structure of carbon, the essential component of living matter. I therefore submitted a block of specially-purified carbon to the influence of the magnetic field. I placed it on the graphite platform and switched on the current, in order to provoke a particular process of disaggregation, which there is no need to explain to you. It was then that the incident occurred that fortuitously revealed the capital virtue of my apparatus.

"Seated facing the platform, with my hands on the switches located in the external face of that marble slab, I was gradually increasing the magnetic flux when a cat slipped into the room through a gap in one of the glass panes in the ceiling. I set about trying to chase it out, but the fleeing animal leapt on to the experimental block of carbon. Oh, my dear Cabri! I heard a *miaow* and...but you'd better see for yourself."

He went out, went to a hutch in a corner of the garden, and came back holding a guinea-pig in his arms.

"Wait here a moment," he said. "I'll go switch on the dynamos."

He handed the animal to me and went into a shed situated some ten paces away.

"Yes," he said, on coming back, "I definitely need a new assistant. I can't do it alone. Let's go back into the laboratory now; I'll reproduce in this guinea-pig the phenomena observed in the cat...for all animals, including all human beings, are equal before the Great Transmutator. That's the name of my apparatus. Now, the experiment!"

V. The Properties of a Colloid

Pitoulet placed the guinea-pig on the graphite platform, climbed up on to the walkway running along the left-hand wall and set himself in front of the big marble console. He operated switches and depressed levers. Then he went to the console set beside the platform and rotated commutators, saying: "20,000 volts. Don't lose sight of the animal."

The latter remained motionless. Suddenly, it uttered a little squeal and made a slight hop, but fell back as if stuck to the platform, and began to subside, collapse and flatten out. Then, its slender legs no longer being able to support it, it spread out like a poultice.

"Stop!" cried Pitoulet, halting the action of the electromagnet. "Do you understand, now, how the cat that paid me a visit became elastic, just like the Bic girl's fox-terrier."

"I understand how," I said, aptly, "but I don't understand why."

"You'll understand why shortly. Let's finish the experiment. From an elastic state, this interesting little animal will become vaporous, if you please. 30,000 volts!"

And he switched the current on again.

"I don't see any change occurring," I said, after a few seconds.

"Wait," he replied. "Although the transition from the solid to the fluid state takes place gradually, that from the fluid state to the vaporous state is instantaneous."

Indeed, a few minutes later, the guinea-pig-poultice swelled up and suddenly rose upwards, transforming itself into a guinea-pig-cloud, rather vague in form but nevertheless recognizable, like a slanting shadow: a form neither diaphanous nor opaque, but smoky, if one might put it like that, with darker internal streaks in which the design of the skeleton was vaguely discernible—and that form, about a meter long and half a meter tall, swayed like a heavy mist above the graphite platform.

"Blow hard, with me," Pitoulet said, stopping the current.

We blew in unison, and the guinea-pig-cloud, expelled from the platform, was thus steered toward the enormous glass bell-jar that I had noticed while walking round the room. Pitoulet attached a cord to the handle at the top, passed the cord over a pulley, raised the bell-jar over the guinea-pig by that means, and then brought it down again upon the animal, thus trapping it inside.

"There it is, caged."

"But is it still alive?"

"Still. You see these three holes pierced in the bell-jar—they let in the air necessary to life."

"But…"

"Patience, impetuous Cabri. Sit down on the walkway with me. For the present, listen."

Then he explained:

"I told you just now that the science that has always excited me most of all is biochemistry. My entire achievement resides in a fortunate application of the laws of electromagnetism to the discoveries of biochemistry. About my part in the invention of the Great Transmutator I have told you all that I can. The rest remains my secret—but it is permissible not to hide anything from you regarding the biochemical conditions of the experiment.

"Every human being, as you probably know, is essentially made up of cells. Now, all these cells, interior protoplasm and walls alike, all the membranes that partition the organism in every direction and all the liquids that bathe it—blood, lymph, chyle, cellular sugar—are constituted by substances that bear the name of colloids. What is a colloid? It is an assembly of ultra-microscopic particles suspended in a liquid medium, which separates and unites them. Organic colloids—in humans, for example—are composed of albuminoid particles about a ten-thousandth of a millimeter large..."

"Small, you mean?" I suggested.

"Large small, as you please. Ten-thousandths of a millimeter are fearfully large compared with millionths of a millimeter. These particles, as I was saying, bathe in a liquid medium, which one might describe, in order to simplify things for your usage, as a saline solution. The human body is nothing but an assemblage of organic colloids. Now, the action of the magnetic field created by the electromagnet has the effect of modifying the consistency of the interposed liquid. In its normal state, that consistency is viscous. The influence of the electromagnet renders it more fluid. To put it another way, the action of the magnetic field has the effect of diminishing the coefficient of viscosity of the interposed liquid. That's quite clear, I imagine.

"What happens in consequence? The particles suspended in the liquid have more freedom of movement, the composite aggregate of the colloid becomes looser, and the consistency of the organism, formerly solid, becomes elastic. Taking the experiment further, however, as I increase the intensity of the magnetic field, the coefficient of viscosity is reduced in proportion, and the primitive liquid, the fluid, becomes vaporous. In addition, the organic particles that originally carried various electric charges, suddenly all acquire the same charge. That's a fact. Now, as everyone knows, two bodies carrying the same electrical charge repel one another. The distance between the particles is therefore enormously increased at a stroke—which is to say that the colloid suddenly passes into a vaporous state, and would pass into the state of a true gas if I increased the intensity of the magnetic field further. The guinea-pig colloid that you see under the bell-jar is, therefore, presently in the state of an organic mist. It would be exactly the same for a human colloid. I think you've understood that.

"The new state lasts for three hours; then a return to the natural state inevitably takes place. I haven't yet succeeded in shortening or extending the duration of the transformation. Thus, for about three hours, the new colloidal state persists without any apparent modification. However, internal processes begin to take effect as soon as the organism is removed from the influence of the magnetic field, and three hours later it reverts to its original state. It is worth noting that the organism must pass through the elastic state in order to attain the vaporous state, but returns directly and abruptly from the vaporous state to the solid state.

"You can now explain, I hope, the phenomena that disconcerted you so much. I found your fiancée's fox-terrier outside my door and, mistaking it for a stray dog, I used it in an experiment. Then I had to go out briefly. On my return I saw, in the street, a series of escaped organic mists. I went back inside so hurriedly that I left my door open. You must have followed close behind me, and came in behind me. In the laboratory, I found my assistant Eusèbe, who was amusing himself by lifting up the bell-jar in which I had enclosed a collection of mist-animals, with all the windows open. The elastic dog had vanished—from what you have told me, the brave animal must have crawled all the way back to its masters.

"When my assistant saw me come in, he fled into the garden. First of all, I tried to catch as many animals as possible in this metallic net; at that moment, I heard footsteps in my house; I remembered that I had left the door open, and it was then that I called out, is alarm: 'Who's there? Close the door, Eusèbe!" On that, you ran away. I called my assistant back mildly, but my decision was irrevocable. His recent misdeed demanded that I get rid of him immediately. He was a very intelligent fellow, but excessively curious and indiscreet. So much the worse for him…."

"You sent him packing?" I asked.

"Yes, completely."

"And you're not afraid that he'll talk?"

"No. I'm perfectly tranquil. He won't talk anymore." On these words, he emitted a short burst of shrill laughter, rather unpleasant, which caused me to shiver slightly.

"You've guessed the rest," he concluded. "My mist-animals spread out in all directions, and, when the time came, resolidified, like the rabbit in your fiancée's home."

"I understand," I declared. "But how do you explain the persistence of life through these changes of state? How do they breathe, eat…and return to nature that which it has given to us?"

"The answer, Cabri, is that the phenomena of digestion are considerably slowed down. The organism experiences no needs of any sort. As for the respiratory functions necessary to life, they continue. Nothing prevents atmospheric gases from penetrating an elastic organism in the ordinary way; as for liquid blood, it circulates easily, the coefficient of viscosity of its constituent colloids is diminished to the same extent as that of all the other parts of the body. In the vaporous state, on the other hand, the circulatory phenomena are modified; circulation is replaced by a particular interaction of organic particles, which I have not yet studied in depth; as for respiration, it becomes a sort of osmosis."

"One more thing, Master. You've mentioned the human organism several times. Have you, therefore, in addition to animal experiments, carried out experiments on humans?"

"Haven't you begun to suspect that 'the elastic hand' was my own hand?"

"Then, at that moment, you were entirely..."

"Entirely elastic. Yes, Cabri. Late yesterday evening, alone in my house, rid of my assistant, I climbed up on to the graphite platform. Like any scientist worthy of the name, I proceeded to experiment on myself."

"And you haven't come to any harm?"

"So little that, for your benefit, I shall do it again."

VI. The Master of the Three States

With that, he headed for the cabinet bearing the inscription *Cloakroom*. As I interrogated him with my gaze, he said: "Clothes don't impede the operation at all, but the magnetic current corrodes them, so it's as well to wear as little as possible. It's also better to take off any rings, watch and chain, etc., whose metal might be profoundly altered. Give me a minute."

He went into the cabinet and returned shortly afterwards. He stepped up on to the walkway and carried out the operations necessary to convey the current on the marble console attached to the wall. Then he climbed up on to the graphite platform.

"Perhaps you haven't noticed this," he said, and showed me a sort of indicator on the inner face of the marble plate next to the platform, on whose dial I saw a needle and two inscribed words: *elastic* and *mist*. "It's a simple electric clock. As the case may be, I place the needle facing the word *elastic* or the word *mist*. As soon as the required state is obtained, the current automatically cuts out. In fact, I won't have the strength any longer to operate the commutators, get down from the platform or maintain the power of the magnetic field. Elastic or mist?"

"If you're going to make a full demonstration, Master, I'll need to see elastic *and* mist."

"So be it. Let's go."

Pitoulet stood upright on the platform; he set the needle to the word *elastic*, manipulated the commutators, and shuddered. His hair stood up slightly; then he seemed to experience a brief nausea. A moment later, he spoke: "The experiment doesn't prevent conversation, except that my voice will become increasing faint and tenuous."

"Tell me what you're experiencing, then, Master."

"A vague, temporary, heartache; at present, I have the impression that something elementary is melting away from me, through all my pores, and that a kind of reduced density is extending through my entire being. It's a very curious sensation of simultaneous lightness and subsidence. Look, my legs are flexing involuntarily...giving way..."

He was obliged to kneel down; his thighs weakened in their turn and he took up a crouching position. I placed myself at his level.

"Everything in me is softening," he continued, "my brain along with everything else. My faculties remain, however; the brain must therefore involve something other than cerebral matter—an interesting contribution to the study of the relationship between body and mind. Can you still hear me well enough?"

"Your voice is getting weaker, Master."

He collapsed on to his belly and subsided further by degrees: a human mollusk.

Suddenly, a bell rang.

"The current has cut out," he told me. "Stand aside a little, please—I'm going to get down."

His arms slid along the platform, and his hands passed over the edge; then they stretched—flowing, as one might say, toward the floor. The arms followed, then the head, then the whole body. And, like the fox-terrier and the guinea-pig, the great scientist began actually to slither. Having covered two meters, he called "Cabri!"—and his voice resembled the bleat of a little lamb. He tried to raise the head that he was maintaining, effortfully, a few centimeters from the floor. I got down on all fours and lent him an ear.

"You'll have to help me curl up in a corner," he said. "We can talk more easily then."

I understood then the full sense of the popular expression "to pick something up spoon-fashion." I picked up that soft mass—proportionately—like a patissier handling dough for a tart, and propped it up, taking care to dispose the hindquarters at the bottom and the head at the top. When the operation as complete, Pitoulet thanked me with a flat smile what seemed to me to be the last word in ridiculousness. It was like looking at a image reflected in an acutely convex mirror.

"Sit down next to me," he said. "You're going to help me in a few experiments that I can't carry out on my own. If you open a cupboard that you'll find in the cabinet, you'll find a funnel, a liter of milk and some eggs. Bring them here."

I obeyed, and, following his instructions, I experimented with the possibility of feeding an elastic organism by pouting milk and raw eggs into his mouth with the aid of the funnel.

"Excellent," he declared. "The aliments zigzag inside me in a most agreeable fashion. Place a newspaper in front of me."

I did so. He read with difficulty, his sight being impeded by excessively flaccid eyelids. His nose remained sensitive to odors. His hearing was ameliorated—by virtue of a fortunate influence of the elastic state, he thought, on the perilymph and the endolymph of the inner ear.

Then I laid him down and stretched out his body to a length of four meters forty. I compacted him again and compressed him into a ball about 50 centimeters in diameter without him experiencing the slightest pain, but he began to choke and I relaxed my grip. His hair remained as it was; his teeth and nails, being slightly harder than the rest of his body, had the texture of rubber.

I was able to exercise all imaginable torsions on his limbs, and plaited his arms together without causing him a moment's discomfort. The parts of the body sustained by the skeleton were a little less soft than the others, and I experienced a stronger resistance in digging my finger into the skull than driving it into the abdomen.

"So you'll stay like this for three hours?" I said.

"No, Cabri, my friend, since you're here. Yesterday I had to spend the night in an elastic state, not being able to stand up or reach the commutators with my arms. But you can put me back on the platform, position the needle on the dial on the word *mist*, and turn the commutators in the direction that I indicate to you—and you'll see me become vaporous."

"Understood, Master. Nevertheless, I wonder how you were able, yesterday, to travel in the elastic state from the laboratory to your bedroom."

"By crawling slowly. Once I had reached my bedroom I wanted to take account of the power of elongation of a part of my body under the effect of gravity. Not without difficulty, I put my hand out of the lowest window, which started flowing down the wall. It was then that you noticed it. It required the greatest effort to bring it back, but I obtained some help from the asperities in the stone, which formed points of support for slithering. After which, I slid into the hollow of a mattress set on the ground in advance, and went to sleep until it was time to become my normal self again. Would you please place me on the platform?"

"Here goes, Master."

Half tugging and half pushing, I hoisted him up on to the apparatus, set the needle to *mist* and restored the current, according to his indications. After a brief interval, I saw him become blurred; within an instant, his body became imprecise, translucent but not transparent, in the fashion of a dirty window-pane. At the same time he grew, until he reached the ceiling, a vast shadow. Then the bell rang.

He advanced toward me. I retreated. Then I heard his minuscule voice, like the mewling of a cat, asking me: "Are you scared? Stand still."

I stopped moving, and Pitoulet passed through me—or, rather, I passed through Pitoulet—without any difficulty; after which, I perceived that a light greasy coating was covering my hands and face. I heard a thin laugh and, cocking my ear toward the ceiling, I perceived the explanation.

"Lipids, otherwise called fats, don't pass completely into the vaporous state, so they leave a slight trace on bodies that pass through them, and your face has just passed through the fattest part of my body. It's an unimportant detail. Transpierce me with that walking-stick."

I passed a cane through his body and met the wall. Then he put his hands on my cheeks; it was like a warmth devoid of contact. He asked me to walk over him, but my feet encountered nothing but the floor. No matter what I did, he remained indivisible, because he was ungraspable.

"This time," he went on, "I'll stay like this for three hours. I don't want to keep you for all that time. You can leave whenever you wish. I don't need anything. The vaporous state is perfectly euphoric."

It was 2 p.m. I kept him company for a while long-er, then went out for a walk, after having promised to come back for dinner.

At 8 p.m., I was there, and I found him resolidified and very cheerful.

"Let's eat!" he cried. "I have a ferocious appetite."

"And everything went smoothly?" I asked.

"Without any hitch. Half an hour before the solidi-fication, one experiences a vague discomfort, both super-ficial and profound, a shrill vibration of the entire being. There's a sort of 'critical point', which coincides with the preliminaries of the return to a normal state. As the internal work of the tissues proceeds, the misty state persists; there's a sudden, instantaneous pain—and it's all over. One finds oneself hale and hearty, as solid as before. Now, it's a matter of impregnating the ensemble of our colloids with old wine. What do you think?"

"I think," I said, sitting down, "that it's an idea of genius, like all of yours, my dear Master, and I remain, facing your discovery, rapt with admiration."

"You're right," he said, not without pride. "I have, in sum, succeeded in provoking a series of changes in organic bodies corresponding to those that are effected on inorganic bodies. One causes inorganic matter to pass between the three states of solid, liquid and gas. I have caused organic matter to pass through its own three states: solid, elastic and vaporous."

"And by virtue of that fact," I proclaimed, raising a glass of Clos-Vougeot to my lips, "you deserve, like all the most illustrious scientists, a sparkling epithet or a glowing nickname, by which your memory will be illu-minated throughout posterity: I drink to *the Master of the Three States*."

And we clinked glasses, our eyes moist with emotion.

VII. Two Nebulous Citizens

Having drunk a toast to *the Master of the Three States*, we drank one to my fiancée, then to Paris, then to Anjou, my native province, then to Brittany, which was his, then to the gracious sovereigns presently visiting the Capital, then to the colloids, and then...with the result that, by the end of the meal, we were enveloped by an aura of beatitude. Pitoulet's nose was scarlet.

"Come on," said my friend, "let's get some fresh air in the garden."

"Get some fresh air." A derisory expression. The air was heavy, without a breath of wind. We breathed with difficulty.

"Do you know what would be delightful?" he said. "A few hours in the vaporous state. One feels light, blissful...no weight in the stomach. I shall offer myself that pleasure. Will you accompany me to the laboratory?"

"Certainly, my dear Master."

Once beside the platform he said to me, smiling: "Will you climb up with me?"

"My word," I replied. "I'm strongly tempted. I won't hide from you that the elastic state doesn't attract me; it renders a man rather grotesque—and when I imagine my Suzanne and I thus metamorphosed, I experience a slight nausea. But the vaporous state seems to me to be distinguished."

"Get undressed, then, and climb up on the platform. Uh oh! Cabri, you're scared!"

"Me, scared? Can a scientific apparatus...?"

"If you aren't scared, Cabri, be less eloquent and more prompt. Get dressed and climb up on the platform."

"I will!"

I went into the cloakroom with him. We came out again naked. "There!" I cried. "Now, *en route* for the land of shadows!"

"How excited the young man is!" said Pitoulet laughing. "there—I've set the needle; I'm starting the current. It's begun!"

Oh, the bizarre sensation! A powerful prickling sensation, profound and total, overwhelmed my body from head to toe. Then I felt as if I were melting, collapsing into myself like a softened block of starch. Pitoulet and I were passing together into the elastic state—but we only passed through it; suddenly we began to grow. It seemed to me that all my organs were swelling up and becoming lighter. My face turned to Pitoulet's, which reached the ceiling of the room; our enormous vaporous looked at one another with a certain emotion. And, as we were on the same level, we were easily able to converse.

"We'll get down," Pitoulet said, "as soon as we hear the bell—and there it is! After you, my dear Cabri. We have three hours before us in the state of human clouds."

We left the platform. He continued: "The door is open. I've got an idea: we'll take a turn around the garden and see how we stand with regard to things."

"Excellent idea," I replied.

We moved around for a little while without tiring of enjoying the most delicate sensations. We walked—or, more accurately, glided—along the pathways, half as tall as the trees whose branches passed through us without any harm being done to them or us. We came upon sleeping birds, and stroked them without waking them up. The intimate perfumes of the high foliage bathed us; we breathed it in, seemingly throughout our entire being, with a delightful facility. In brief, the vaporous state was accompanied by a general delight, doubtless due to our lightness—for, according to Pitoulet's calculations, we weighed scarcely twice as much as the volume of air we displaced.

Thus walking and chatting, we came to the end of the garden, and looked to see what was happening in the neighboring houses. Invisible in the darkness, we looked through the windows at many a spectacle that gave us pleasure.

"Another time," Picoulet said, "you can shut me up, while in a vaporous state, in a thin sealed container. You can compress me without effort to the volume of a large melon. Nothing's easier, if one wants to travel incognito, that to have oneself transported by a friend in the guise of a child's balloon."

"I imagine so!" I exclaimed. "If only I could steal my Suzanne away from her parents by means of that artifice. I could carry her in compressed form, in my bosom!"

"Don't worry about that," he replied. "I've thought about it, and I've found 19 ways of getting her back."

"Oh, Master—you're my savior!"

"Would you like to test out the first means that I think excellent?"

"Do you need to ask?"

"Well, here it is. The street is deserted. Not a breath of air. I'll go out and appear before the spouses Bic as the spirit of an ancestor, who commands them to give you their daughter."

"Genius! Madame Bic has an iron-hard belief in spiritualism—and, in the intimacy of their home, she dominates her husband. It's to her that you should appear."

"What's her grandfather's name?"

"Gédéon Mornebler, a dealer in birds from the Isles. But can't I go with you?"

"Yes indeed, Cabri; the two of us will knock them dead."

"Nevertheless, Master," I added, "I'd like the scene to take place in the absence of my dear Suzanne, She's as sensitive as the clematis of the fields, and I fear…"

"We'll wait for the old people to be alone."

Brave Pitoulet! He spoke of "old people," although he was old himself, with the soul of a young man.

After discussing all the possible contingencies, we climbed over the garden wall and fell down into the street again like scarves of gauze—gas, I would risk, if I did not have to refrain, along with the great Victor Hugo (who did not always deprive himself of the privilege) from "the droppings of an airborne spirit."[20]

---

[20] Unsurprisingly, the intricacy of the wordplay in the original of this passage does not translate easily into English, although the similarity between *gaze* [gauze] and *gaz* [gas] does not disappear entirely. In *Les Misérables* (1862)—which, as its title suggests, is not exactly a barrel of laughs—Victor Hugo passes aphoristic judgment on punning with the harsh judgment that *"le calembour est la fiente de l'esprit qui vole"* [puns are the faeces of soaring wit]. Cabri's appropriation takes some advantage of a double entendre within the aphorism, which permits *esprit* to be construed as "spirit" instead of "wit,",but the initial reference likening his descent from the garden wall to the dropping of a gauze scarf also implies a subtler pun with respect to Hugo's terminology; when a lady

And here we are on the sidewalk. Not a breath of wind. We advance, colossal shadows, slightly overlapping—and after a few meters we see a young couple coming toward us, tenderly enlaced. As Pitoulet has foreseen, we are confused with the evening mist. Moreover, the lovers are scarcely occupied with the external world. They pass right through us without suspecting it, their lips united. Nevertheless—our hearing being very sensitive—we hear the girl say to the boy: "Don't you think, Gustave, that our kiss had a funny taste? It seemed as if I had grease on my lips?"

"I had the same impression, Isabelle," he replies.

In fact, their two faces have passed through our bellies. Then we cross the path of three artillerymen who are marching as if in a dream. They do not perceive us. We have almost arrived when an old lady on the opposite sidewalk undoubtedly sees us silhouetted by the light of a gas-lamp, for she points at the street-light with a squeal of alarm. Already, though, we have leapt over the garden wall of Castel Bic.

It was important now to act boldly and prudently. The night was dark. By bending down we were able to look in through the open window of the dining room, which was illuminated. Monsieur Bic, his pipe between his lips, was reading a newspaper. Madame Bic was knitting. My Suzanne was leaning through a book, but her beautiful eyes often looked up at the ceiling, pensively. A little while later, she left the room. Was she

---

deliberately drops a scarf in order that a gentleman in whom she is interested might pick it up and return it, such an action qualifies as a *feinte* [ploy], a word that can be modified by a transposition of letters into *fiente*, which I have elected to translate in the text, with due delicacy, as "droppings."

going to return? We made a tour of the house and saw her bedroom light go on. She got undressed. There was a blue nightgown lying on a chair beside her. Oh, how I would have loved to satiate my gaze on the charming spectacle of that state of undress! Pitoulet reminded me of the situation.

"Let's not waste time—this is the moment."

I tore myself away from that enchanted place with difficulty, and we went back to the dining room. We heard the sounds of a mandolin; my Suzanne was giving voice to her harmonious melancholy—which did not prevent Bic from declaring: "Our daughter is playing false notes."

The Barbarian! The notes, false or not, added the attraction of an unexpected morbidity to the nostalgic ballad. But it was necessary to get to work. Simultaneously, Pitoulet and I went through the window into the room, and we crouched down, him in front of Madame and me in front of Monsieur.

In our faint, shrill voices, we gave orders: "Not a gesture. Not a sound. Your lives depend on it."

In the lamplight, our enormous vaporous faces were clearly distinguishable. The spouses Bic started in unison and swallowed the cries ready to emerge from their open mouths. Bic dropped his pipe. Madame Bic put her hands together fearfully.

Pitoulet started immediately. "Clothilde Bic, I am the Spirit of your grandfather Gédéon Mornebler. I have come back on this memorable evening to tell you that I am watching over you, and to communicate my wishes. I order you and your spouse to marry your daughter to Mesmin Cabri, whose astral double I have evoked."

"Present!" I said to Monsieur Bic.

"Returned briefly from the Empire of Souls, I foresee, spouses Bic, that if your daughter marries him, you will all live long and prosperous lives. If not, then misfortune and damnation will be upon you all—misfortune and damnation!"

Pitoulet prophesied with the assurance of a professional revenant. He added: "You shall write a letter to Mesmin this very evening, and you will marry him to Suzanne within the month." He addressed himself to me: "I give you warning of that, astral double!"

"Duly noted, Spirit of Mornebler!" I replied, respectfully.

"And now," he concluded, "swear to obey me, Bics!"

"I swear," stammered Madame, curled over in fright.

Bic remained silent, rolling his eyes anxiously…but we heard my Suzanne's footsteps; we disappeared through the open window, but remained on watch in the shadows.

"I think the effect was successful," Pitoulet whispered.

"Let's wait and see," I murmured, anxiously.

On seeing her dumbfounded parents, Suzanne said, anxiously: "Papa! Mama! What's the matter? Tell me! You're frightening me!"

Bic leapt to his feet and leaned out of the window. Naturally, he saw nothing. He went back, muttering: "Some illusion…I've drunk too much coffee."

"What about me?" said his wife. "Too much lime-tea, perhaps?"

"There's something behind this…"

"There's the will of my grandfather Mornebler behind it. Face it—you saw him as clearly as you see me!"

"Grandpapa Gédéon?" Suzanne queried. "What do you mean?"

"Don't be afraid, my child," her mother replied. "Your father and I will discuss it. Is Monsieur Mesmin still to your liking?"

Only a maternal heart has such delicacy. Suzanne lowered her head and murmured: "Oh, yes!"

If Pitoulet had not restrained me, she would have received a shadow's embrace.

"Very well," her mother replied, "You shall marry him when you…"

VIII. A Gala at the Opéra

We would have loved to know more, but a light breeze sprang up, which blew us away from the window.

"Oh!" said Pitoulet. "Wind's the last thing we need. And here's the Moon showing its face. Let's get back to the laboratory."

"Let's get back," I agreed.

Lifted up by the breeze, we passed over the wall at a slightly greater height than was necessary, and fell back into the street. There, a surprise awaited us; the wind, which had been blowing gently between the enclosing walls of the garden, strengthened more briskly in the corridor of the street, in a direction exactly opposite to the one we needed to take.

A few seconds sufficed for us to observe, anxiously, that instead of advancing we were retreating rather rapidly. Like swimmers exhausting themselves by struggling against a current bearing them away from the bank, we exhausted ourselves resisting the wind that was drawing us away from the haven. I was horribly anxious. We were forced, after a short time, to turn around, with our backs to the wind, in order not to continue retreating blindly. In less than three minutes, it pushed us all the way to the end of the street, on to the Quai de Passy, and into a coaching entrance. There, we were sheltered.

"Well," I said to Pitoulet, who was huddling under the archway like me, "here's a nice situation."

"Let's wait for a calm," he replied.

I gazed along the Seine, and observed that the Alexandre III bridge, and the Grand and Petit Palais, were all lit up. "Look," I said to Pitoulet.

"Why so many lights?" he said.

"Have you forgotten that Paris is entertaining royal visitors?"[21]

"Unimportant..."

We prick up our ears. Behind the glazed door that closed the archway on the side of the courtyard, footsteps and voices can be heard. Dreading that an abrupt current of air might tear us apart, we decide to go out, inasmuch as the wind seems to us to have weakened—but whoosh! The westerly wind, actually more violent, drags us away in its course. It is at the speed of a trotting horse that we go along the pier toward the Place de la Concorde, in an oppressive silence.

Level with the Pont de l'Alma, the groups of strollers become frequent and dense, and the pier is brightly lit. Thus, in spite of the rapidity of our passage, we are immediately noticed. I shall not undertake to record the greater number of the exclamations that are uttered: some people collapse in fear, others stand there stupefied, others follow our course, and the most courageous throw stones at us—which, without doing us the slightest harm, strike people in the vicinity. Others, alerted by the rumor and the screams, run to meet us, passing through us and colliding violently with our pursuers.

---

[21] Falk appears to be taking liberties with chronology here. The reader might well have deduced (and subsequent data will support the implication) that a little more than a year has now elapsed since the date of Cabri's initial qualification in Law, and that it is the beginning of August 1914, on the eve of the formal outbreak of the Great War, but the reference to royal visitors in Paris is suggestive of that year's state visit of King George V and Queen Mary, which actually took place in April.

In brief, as we reach the Place de la Concorde, the tumult becomes so loud that a brigade of policemen, posted in the courtyard of the Bourbon Palace, think it a manifestation of unrest and start striking out with their fists—an intervention that gives rise to a perfect brawl.

Amid the curses of men, the groans of women and the weeping of children, we were flying on at high speed, tracked by the policemen and our fellow citizens, when an opportunity was offered to us: the gate of the Jardin des Tuileries was closed. We slipped between the bars; the howling mob crushed itself against them, and thus lost track of us.

Beneath the trees the wind calmed down, and our moderated velocity permitted us to exchange a few impressions.

"We're rather a long way from Auteuil," I observed.

"Oh, my poor Cabri! Just as long as we don't fall into the Seine! And as long as it doesn't rain!"

"What would happen?"

"I don't know. Perhaps we'd be seriously dissociated, disaggregated by the rain…"

"You might have told me that sooner!"

But the wind gets up again; our speed increases. A flash of light: the Rue de Castiglione. Then there's the Place du Carrousel, scintillating with electric globes. There, a brisk and powerful gust of wind blasts us through the gates, so forcefully that in less than a minute, here we are in the Avenue de l'Opéra, resplendent with 1000 lights. Black clouds are galloping across the sky, and we are galloping as rapidly as they are, There too, the crowd is not slow to notice our passage, and the scenes of the Place de la Concorde are repeated, increased in violence. The police, doubtless thinking it some anarchist plot, precipitate themselves forward with sabers drawn, while the mounted policemen make their horses dance. Howls, insults, battles…and the pursuit of the two phantoms pushed by the wind toward the Opéra, entirely bathed in blue light, the balconies of which are decked with red velvet carpets fringed with gold—the Opéra, where a gala reception is being given for his sovereign friends by the President of the French Republic!

A hope is mingled with my fear, however, for the Opéra is an enclosed space: a refuge, perhaps salvation. The wind is driving us toward the doors. O joy! One of them is open! We pass through the cordon of guards standing in front of the steps—who, their eyes directed toward the movement of the crowd, hardly notice our entry.

Without taking time to observe the scene that must be unfolding behind us, we penetrate into the vestibule, where a few ushers take fright, and, now masters of our direction, we leap from floor to floor, while the noise of hurrying footsteps and harsh argumentative voices decreases in our ears. In less than a minute, we find ourselves huddled in a dark redoubt at the summit of the edifice.

After a moment of relieved silence, we consult one another:

"Where are we?" Pitoulet asks.

"I don't know."

"Did anyone see us come in?"

"It's possible."

"Do you know what time it is?"

"10:30 p.m. by the clock on the Boulevard."

"I suspected as much," he replied. "Can't you feel a sort of internal vibration, which involves intermittent stabbing sensations that are quite painful?"

"Yes indeed. So what?"

"So, in approximately half an hour we'll resolidify."

"Thank Heaven! Let it come, the moment of liberation! I've had enough of the vaporous state."

"Keep it down Cabri, I beg you."

At that moment, we were interrupted by the unleashed racket of the orchestra. Presumably the performance was starting up again, after an interval. We were apparently in a part of the theater close to the stage, since we could hear the music so clearly. But where? In that dark place, we listened to duets, mixed choirs and sometimes to polite—very slight—applause.

Suddenly, the little nook lit up, and we realized that we were in a costume-store. Intruders were undoubtedly about to arrive; soft footfalls were already hastening. The door at the rear was open; we went out and wandered, troubled phantoms, through a labyrinthine series of corridors, and eventually heard the orchestra launch into the ballet from *Faust*. At the same time, we arrived at a long iron gallery bordered by a guard-rail; at the far end of the gallery scene-shifters were at work. Our head were touching the ceiling of the theater.

I realized that the gallery was the central arch when I saw the stage down below—far below—where a company of dancers was twirling. But sandaled scene-shifters, arriving from the direction of the circle, set out along the gallery, moving toward us. Pitoulet and I leaned over to see whether there was any exit in the direction of the garden. Presumably we leaned over a little too far, for—the guard-rail having no existence for us—we fell off the arch and began to descend, slowly, from the ceiling to the stage below.

How can I describe what happened next? We landed, immense foggy bales, beneath the convergence of multicolored spotlights, smack in the middle of the waltz from *Faust*, initially unnoticed by the whirlwind of dancers, who were entirely focused on their entrechats. Our appearance caused a certain disturbance in the auditorium and the orchestra, though—as is, I assume, easily believable. A murmur emanated from the musicians and the public, as indefinable as the apparition itself: a murmur that was prevented by official convention from mounting as far as exclamation.

Soon, a few dancers perceived that bizarre clouds were interposing themselves between them. A malaise, pregnant with catastrophe, hung in the air—a brief malaise, for the catastrophe burst forth, even more horrible than might have been expected. All of a sudden, it was no longer two phantoms that were mingled with the frolics of the dancers but—time having moved on—two flesh-and-blood individuals: two lamentable individuals at the extreme of humiliation, indecency and ridicule, irredeemably naked!

The orchestra, after a discordant crash, fell silent. Howling dancers ran away. The hall reverberated with protests.

We had time to see the President rise to his feet and the curtain fall, and that was all. An avalanche of blows, delivered by fists, canes and boots, fell upon Pitoulet and me. In the blink of an eye, we found ourselves wrapped up in sheets and, trussed up like sausages, thrown in the back of a taxi.

Ten minutes later, we were introduced, under strong escort, into the Commissariat.

IX. Trypax and Larigoule

The Police Commissioner was a man with a crimson complexion, thick close-cropped hair the color of a crow's wing, bushy eyebrows, a thick moustache, jet-black eyes and shiny pointed teeth. A thick red neck protruded from the flared collar of his shirt, and his clenched fists, posed on his desk, were menacing even at rest. Beside him, a thin, round-shouldered man, pale and blond, with a thin moustache and soft cheeks, was poised to start writing, by the light of an oil-lamp.

The Commissioner listened to the report of the brigadier, his eyebrows coming together on his furrowed brow in a terrible manner. At the same time, he drilled us with his gaze, as black as his heart. The report said, approximately, that: "two non-qualified fanatics, dressed only in the attributes of nature, had sprung forth, without any functional reason, within the *corps de ballet* of the Opéra, occasioning a great perturbation in the military and civil personnel at the performance; that the representatives of public authority hidden behind the scenery had leapt on to the stage preventatively and reduced the delinquents to helplessness and modesty, by wrapping them up in skillfully-improvised materials."

"Very well," articulated the Commissioner. Addressing his agents, he added: "Search them!"

We were stripped of our bonds and wrapping. How many hiding places the simple human body conceals, in the suspicions of the police! Unimaginable! Pitoulet could not believe his eyes.

"Hidden objects: total, none," declared the brigadier.

"That's good," pronounced the Commissioner. To us he said: "Get dressed!"

Get dressed! Irony! Eventually, we draped ourselves as best we could, me in a heliotrope mantle, probably part of Faust's costume, and Pitoulet in a red cape, doubtless belonging to Mephisto, which had appropriately constituted our packaging.

"You, the old one!" thundered the Commissioner. "Your name, forenames, profession, age and address. Ready, Beauléon?"

"Yes, Monsieur Trypax," the secretary replied.

"Pitoulet, Jules-César-Guy, rentier, 63 years old, resident of Auteuil, 68 Rue de La Fontaine.

"You, the young one!"

"Cabri, Mesmin-Justin, 25 years old, advocate's clerk, 97 Avenue des Ternes."

"Can you explain the facts? You first, Pitoulet?"

I would never have suspected that a scientist of such genius would reveal himself to be so devoid of imagination at such a moment—for I understood immediately that he wanted to hide the truth. He stood there for a moment, mute, scanning all of us with wild eyes, and then he stammered, somewhat ridiculously: "It was an unfortunate coincidence."

"Thunder!" swore the Commissioner, thumping his desk hard enough to crack a nut. "I need an answer, not a commentary. What were you doing, in a state of nudity, accompanied by your acolyte, in the Académie Nationale de la Musique?"

Pitoulet remained silent. I tried to speak.

"Shut up!" howled Trypax. "I'm talking to the old cretin."

At that moment, the door opened, giving passage to a gentleman in a suit and top hat. The furious Trypax immediately became gracious.

"Monsieur Larigoule! Come in, I beg you."

I thought I remembered that Larigoule was the name of an important official in the Sûreté.

The visitor replied, in an amiable tone: "Don't disturb yourself. Continue your interrogation." Then he leaned over the scribe's shoulder and added, smiling: "I see that it hasn't got very far."

"It's this old cretin, who's stubbornly..."

For a few seconds, I inclined all my mental powers toward the elaboration of an acceptable story. I suddenly stifled a joyful "Eureka!" Decorating my face with the most wining of smiles, I began: "Monsieur le Grand Inspecteur en Chef..."

I was not entirely clear about Larigoule's rank, so I conferred upon him a title that, if not real, was at least flattering.

"Shut up!" roared Trypax.

"If he wants to talk, let's listen, my dear chap," said Larigoule, softly. "Cabri, Mesmin, advocate's clerk?"

"Qualified in Law, Monsieur le Grand Inspecteur. That tells you that I'm not a vagabond, any more than my venerable friend is. You see in us the sorry victims of a rather unfortunate adventure, for which we should not bear, civilly or criminally, the responsibility."

Larigoule looked at me, smiling, and I understood that his affability was more dangerous than Trypax's brutality.

Draped in our capes, we bowed in a dignified manner.

At the same time, I perceived dread and supplication in Pitoulet's eyes. I continued without delay, in order to reassure him.

"This is what happened. During the heat wave, my old friend Pitoulet, who lives, so to speak, in the country, invited me to stay with him. Now, with all his virtues, he's afflicted with a constitutional vice that he strongly desires to keep secret, but which I'm forced to reveal to you. He is subject to fits of somnambulism. This evening, after going to bed at 9:30 p.m., as usual, he got up, prey to one of these fits. As I was lodged in the next room, I heard him go out of his room and I followed him, without waking him up, for, as you know, nothing is more dangerous than waking a sleep-walker— especially if he's an old man—at the risk of killing him on the spot. So, Pitoulet opened the door and set out into the street. I tried several times to make him turn round, but he was blindly and obstinately following a determined direction. I had to limit myself to guiding him, in order to prevent him being knocked down by cars. He went down to the river, went over the Pont d'Iéna through the Jardins du Trocadéro, along the Avenue du Trocadéro as far as the Etoile, along the Avenue de Friedland and the Boulevard Haussmann, and went to the Opéra, with me still following, through the stage door..."

Larigoule half-closed his eyelids. He said to me, in a slightly mocking tone: "And no one stopped you as you went in?"

"No one."

"One question, young man. Explain your absence of clothing."

"That's extremely simple. It was so hot, this evening, in Auteuil, that we had decided to sleep entirely nude. When Pitoulet went out, under the influence of his fit, I was obliged to follow him without getting dressed, for fear of losing track of him."

"Bizarre. Truly bizarre!"

"Implausible!" bellowed Trypax.

"The truth," I insinuated, delicately, "can sometimes…"

"Agreed," conceded Larigoule, "but what surprises me most of all is that, in the course of this excursion, you didn't run into anyone."

"We did run into people."

"And no one took any notice of you?"

"No one."

"Not even the police?"

Without replying, I sketched a gesture of ignorance that was, I confess, a trifle disingenuous.

"And in the theater itself, you circulated without crossing the path of seamstresses, employees, stagehands, or any other personnel?"

"We crossed the paths of numerous personnel."

"But no one questioned you?"

"No one."

"How did you get on to the stage?"

"By passing through two doorways. I tried, in vain, to hold Pitoulet back—but I followed him to the end, fearing that he might fall into the orchestra-pit. Our sudden arrest woke him up. He was very surprised to find that he was not in his bed."

"Oh, yes!" Pitoulet agreed, doubtless even more surprised by my inventive genius.

Trypax bit his knuckles; Larigoule remained thoughtful. Then, addressing Pitoulet, he said: "And you, what have you to say?"

"Nothing," my friend stammered. "I was surprised...very surprised..."

Silence fell.

"There's a mystery here," Larigoule concluded. "You haven't told the whole story."

"I beg your pardon..."

"Or your story is false from start to finish. But the police were at fault, I admit, since, until the moment of your appearance, you had been ignored. We shall set out to clarify the affair. Whatever ensues, you have explained yourselves, and your statements will be put on record. You can go home, both of you. Trypax, you will have these gentlemen accompanied, in order to verify their addresses."

"Certainly, Monsieur Larigoule." He addressed himself to us. "Countersign your statements. Good. Don't forget that you both remain at my disposal."

Draped in our capes, we bowed in a dignified manner.

"Go with them, Brigadier Grandcoeur."

The brigadier showed us out and summoned a policeman, who hailed a cab. All four of us set out for the Rue La Fontaine, the policeman alongside the driver and the brigadier facing us. We maintained silence, but in the shadows I felt Pitoulet's hand squeeze mine.

With the aid of crude ploys, the brigadier tried to trip us up. Poor fellow! We smiled at him pityingly. Finally, we arrived. As we were about to get down he held us back "Wait a minute. Percot, proceed with your verbal inquiry."

The policeman rang the doorbell, but Pitoulet called out: "There's no one in!"

"Have you the key, then?" asked the brigadier.

I looked at Pitoulet anxiously. He simply replied: "No." I shivered. Doubtless desirous of producing his own little effect on me, however, he added: "No...but you'll find it by lifting up that stone next to the door."

The policeman bent down and lifted the stone. A key was lying there, which opened the door.

"Do I need to describe the interior of my house?" asked Pitoulet, haughtily.

The policemen looked at one another. "No need," declared the brigadier. "You're home, all right. *Au revoir*, Messieurs...if you'd like to pay the fare."

"What!" Our first movement was to search for our pockets. The policemen burst out laughing. "Since you're home," the brigadier suggested to Pitoulet, slyly, "go get some money."

"That's a bit much!"

Pitoulet went in, came back with some money, and paid the coachman majestically. The policemen, convinced, drew away and we finally went into the dear little house that we had thought we might never see again, full of emotion.

X. Castel Bic

When the door was duly closed again on the police, my worthy Master and I, seized by a sudden impulse, threw ourselves into one another's arms.

"Alone at last!" we exclaimed, at the same time.

"Ah, my dear Cabri," Pitoulet went on, with a joyful sigh, "we've had a lucky escape!"

"I'm terribly hungry, my worthy Master!"

We had a substantial cold snack, went to close up the laboratory, and went to bed. We soon fell into a peaceful and deep sleep.

The following morning, as soon as we found ourselves back in the dining room in front of two bowls of hot chocolate, Pitoulet came toward me with his hands extended.

"To think that I forgot to thank you, yesterday, and to congratulate you on your presence of mind! Your sleepwalking story worked wonders."

"Yes," I replied, modestly, "it wasn't bad. Don't be deceived, though—I don't think we're finished with the curiosity of the police."

"Oh, my God!"

"Fortunately," I said, laughing, "they're not only thinking about us…"

The doorbell rang loudly. Pitoulet, almost fainting, supported himself on the furniture, and I stopped laughing. Gudule came in.

"A telegram for Monsieur Cabri."

I had asked my concierge to forward my correspondence to Pitoulet's address. I opened the folded sheet, read it, and uttered a cry of joy. "Listen, my worthy Master!" And I read aloud:

Dear Monsieur Mesmin,

The manner in which we sent you away the other evening appears to us, on reflection, a trifle precipitate. Come to lunch tomorrow at Castel Bic. Our Suzanne instructs me to tell you that she will be happy to see you again. Cordially,

Pancrace Bic.

"O joy! O joy!" I cried. "There's the result of our nocturnal visit. It's my turn to thank you, with all my gratitude, great and worthy Master! You'll excuse me for not dining with you?"

"Only too happy to have repaired a misunderstanding of which I was the cause."

The housekeeper came in again, the newspapers in her hand. I unfolded one of them feverishly. On the first column of the second page, we read:

An incident momentarily disturbed the gala performance at which our august guests were in attendance. Two theater employees, under the influence of the excitement caused by the presence of the sovereigns, irrupted on to the stage in a state of undress to take part in the ballet from Faust. They were immediately expelled. The incident did not prevent Their Majesties from enjoying the rest of the performance, for which they did not spare their august applause; they called the Director of the Opéra into their box, congratulated him warmly, and awarded him the Order of Choreographical Merit. Afterwards they retired, accompanied by the Head of State, visibly delighted by their evening.

We opened other papers; they all contained the same article, evidently fed to them.

"You can see by this communiqué," I said to Pitoulet, "that the matter is settled. The affair has been covered up. This preposterous story of drunken sceneshifters demonstrates the difficulty the police have found in explaining the inexplicable."

"So much the better, thank God!" he sighed.

On turning more pages, however, we found a few articles related to the pursuit of the phantoms, these very various, demonstrating the extent to which the same event can be reported differently by its witnesses.

One journalist wrote:

Yesterday evening, at about 10 p.m., on the piers, the crowds of strollers were able to witness a curious meteorological phenomenon. Two clouds vaguely affecting human form ran along, skimming the ground, and dissipated shortly afterwards. A few accidents were caused by the jostling as everyone ran to see the phenomenon.

Another wrote:

A certain quantity of heavy vapor escaped from a factory in Billancourt, and rolled along the piers in spirals yesterday evening. A few people were inconvenienced, but rapidly-administered first aid was able to counter the onset of asphyxia.

Yet another:

The Avenue de l'Opéra was the theater of a brief scuffle yesterday evening. A few people having cried "Ghosts!" the entire crowd, prey to a collective hallucination, thought it could see ghosts in a layer of mist produced by the heat: a further example of the imitative spirit of crowds, which the great psychologist Alfred Tarde would certainly have recorded in his immortal work.[22]

And another:

A few practical jokers let off fireworks yesterday evening in the Avenue de l'Opéra, in spite of the official prohibition. A thick smoke was emitted, causing a slight panic. The authors of this stupid joke have been taken to the police cells.

"There we go," I said, putting down the papers. "You can sleep easy. The main thing is that no reporter thought of making a connection between the phantoms in the street and the theater grotesques. On that, permit me to take my leave…"

"When shall I see you again?"

"I shall come back to shake you by the hand later in the day."

And I went home swiftly, in order to put on a seductive outfit.

On coming back to the Rue La Fontaine at midday, I did not notice anything abnormal in the vicinity of Pitoulet's house, and, filled with radiant emotion, with a

---

[22] This reference is mistaken; it was actually Alfred Tarde's father, Gabriel Tarde, who introduced the notion that crowds might be considered as being possessed of a "collective mind," which was greatly elaborated by Gustave Le Bon.

bouquet of white roses in my hand, I rang the doorbell at the threshold of paradise.

Bic offered me a rough friendly hand-shake; I kissed Madame Bic's hand as she contemplated me with a fearful expression, which I pretended not to notice. Suzanne appeared, accompanied by Fredaine. I gave her my bouquet and had the joy of depositing an ardent kiss on her forehead, while my hands gripped hers.

I exclaimed, gaily: "He's better then, the little fox-terrier! I've thought long and hard about the adventure and found the explanation of the phenomenon that brought your criticism down upon me. He was ill, the poor dear, and, although I had been sent away, I should have come back with a veterinarian."

"It was, at any rate, a strange malady," Suzanne replied. "But he got better all on his own. Shortly after your departure, he resumed his natural form."

"You see, my dear, that I had nothing to do with it."

"I beg your pardon…"

Our amorous gazes met.

"As for the rabbit," I went on, after a pleasant pause, "it simply came in through the window…"

The parents Bic were listening to me; from the corner of my eye, I saw the mother, behind her daughter, shake her head dubiously, with a sigh.

We sat down to lunch; in the course of the meal I showed sparkling wit and verve, and sensed that Suzanne adored me more than ever.

On the other hand, I understood that her parents were nursing questions that they dared not ask in front of her. I was, therefore, unsurprised to see them make an excuse send Suzanne away after lunch, and go to enormous lengths to bring the conversation round to the nocturnal occurrence, without appearing to do so.

"Did you sleep well last night?" Madame Bic asked me.

"Certainly," I replied. "Why?"

"It's just that we dreamed about you," said her husband. "We saw you in a dream."

"I'm very flattered."

"And we thought, perhaps," his wife went on, "that you might perhaps have dreamed about us, by virtue of telepathy."

"I confess that I did not," I riposted, "but if I had been able to do so, it would have been a pleasure."

"There are such bizarre circumstances," she continued, with a deep sigh, "of a telepathic order. One often sees friends, distant relative, even dead ones…"

"In dreams?" I said, ingenuously.

"In dreams, or even in a waking state."

"By evocation, then," I said, very seriously. "I have seen spirit apparitions provoked by mediums. If the question interests you, I can recommend some good authors: Boirac, Richet, Colonel de Rochas…"[23]

"Are there also spontaneous apparitions," Madame Bic asked.

"They have been cited."

"What about 'doubles'? What are 'doubles,' exactly?"

"I can see, dear Madame," I said, bowing, "that the vocabulary of spiritism has no secrets for you. 'Doubles'

---

[23] Falk probably had not had an opportunity to read Emile Boirac's *L'Avenir des Sciences Psychiques* (1917) before writing "Le Maître des trois états," and remembered the name from the preface cited in the note attached to the previous story. Charles Richet (1850-1935) was a biologist who also worked in the field of psychic research.

are the imperishable astral envelopes of mortal terrestrial beings. We each have our double. When we disappear, it survives us and becomes our 'spirit.' But this is a big subject, and I fear…"

"Oh, do continue!" begged Madame Bic, hanging on my every word.

Solemnly, I replied: "There are grave matters therein, about which it is not appropriate to talk without precaution." I lowered my voice, adopting an emotional and mock-fearful tone: "Then again, if it is necessary to tell you everything, some of my friends have already seen my 'double' and—between ourselves—I don't like to talk about it."

Zap! Bang on the nose! The two spouses shuddered, and exchanged a long glance. Madame Bic made a gesture, and apparent precursor of a confession—but she doubtless did not dare.

Suzanne reappeared. The conversation ended there. My fiancée and I returned to the pathways of the garden for a sentimental promenade. When I left her, I swore to come to see her again the following day.

XI. An Escape of Gas

Alone in the street, I remembered that I had promised to visit Pitoulet. As I approached his house I saw a little crowd gathered outside his door. I pressed my pace, but before going in, I lent an ear to what the idlers were saying

I heard:

"The police are in the house."

"The Commissioner is having it searched."

"They're going to arrest the old maniac."

"He's running an illicit still."

I pushed through the crowd and bumped into two policemen, who forbade me to enter.

"Is it Monsieur Trypax who's in charge?" I asked.

"Yes," they replied, astonished.

"Go tell your master that Monsieur Cabri is at the door. You'll see whether he'll have me let in immediately."

"I'm not saying anything different," said one of the policemen, suddenly respectful. "My colleague will take you to him."

Accompanied by the policeman, I went into the scientist's study, where I found Trypax and Pitoulet face to face, the former crimson and more thunderous than ever, the latter pale and bewildered. My old friend greeted me with the gaze of a shipwreck-victim perceiving a rock.

Trypax greeted me with: "You've arrived just in time!"

The policeman, satisfied, went away. The Commissioner went on: "I was just about to have you picked up at your home."

"A needless trouble," I said, with pursed lips. "You can see that I'm not in hiding."

"There's nothing to be got out of the old cretin—but you, you're going to give me some answers."

"Pardon!"

In the delight that an excellent lunch and the joy of seeing Suzanne again had plunged me, I felt my dialectical faculties multiplied tenfold, and to avoid replying, I asked: "Am I being charged with something, by any chance?"

"No, but…"

"Am I to be called as a witness?"

"Not that either, but…"

"In any case, I'm as anxious as you are to be informed immediately. My deposition would be inoperative, for I am Monsieur Pitoulet's legal adviser, having taken responsibility for his interests. So, you've come to carry out a search?"

"Exactly. I have a warrant from the Investigating Magistrate. I have in my possession, moreover, a very interesting legal statement that my local colleague has communicated to me. Either I'm much mistaken, or Monsieur Pitoulet is the perpetrator who has infested the buildings in the neighborhood with various birds and mammals. I'm beginning to see what's going on!" He laughed ferociously, and shouted: "Beauléon!"

The secretary approached.

"Go and inspect the furniture," Trypax said, "and prepare seals for anything that seems suspicious. You, Pitoulet, take me to your laboratory."

"My labobo…"

"Exactly. You'll see that I know how to conduct an investigation. You're pulling the strings of some apparatus or other in a vast laboratory. Let's go."

How could we resist? The priest of science guided the profaner to the threshold of his sanctuary. I followed them. We went in, and Pitoulet closed the door. We were in front of the Great Transmutator again.

"What do you do with all this?" Trypax demanded.

In the presence of his machine, the inventor, as if inflated by parental pride, recovered his voice. "*All this*," he replied, in an almost arrogant tone, "is used in my experiments."

"What experiments?"

He murmured "*Margaritas ante porcum,*"[24] and continued: "Experiments related to certain problems in chemistry and physics."

"What problems?"

Trypax's insistence was visibly exasperating him. "That's my secret," he replied.

"There are no secrets from the police. I demand that you say what the problems are."

Pitoulet's nose went white, which seemed to me to be a sign of impending fury. After a pause, during which he seemed to reflect, I heard him reply, to my great surprise: "The problem of seeing through opaque bodies. When one climbs on to that platform and I start the machine working, one can see through walls."

As curious as he was authoritarian, Trypax leapt on to the platform and ordered: "Switch the machine on."

"Willingly."

With a diabolical smile, Pitoulet turned his manual controls and levers.

---

[24] Pearls before swine.

"I can't see anything," Trypax complained.

"Wait—you'll see."

"Oh! What! Oh! What's happening to me? Stop! I want to get down."

"You'd do better to remain calm."

And Pitoulet, snatching my walking-stick, pushed Trypax back on to the platform with a thrust of the handle. An instant later, his softening legs refused the enemy any further service; his body subsided, his voice weakened; he uttered moaning cries of "Help!" imperceptible from outside, and looked at us with round, terrified eyes.

"The full current!" Pitoulet exclaimed.

The agglutinate of colloids that constituted a Commissioner flattened before our eyes. The corpulent Trypax, like a giant frog, tried to jump off the platform, exhaling in a hoarse purr: "Murderer! Bandit! Stop!"

"On the contrary! Full current!"

And with his cane, Pitoulet maintained him on the platform. Soon, Trypax collapsed completely, and suddenly passed from the elastic state into the vaporous state: he became the giant shadow that no longer has any secrets for the reader. I expected to see the experiment stop there. Not at all! Suddenly, that shadow was effaced; the mist vanished and nothing—absolutely nothing—any longer remained of Trypax on the platform of the machine.

"Pitoulet!" I cried, astounded. "What have you done?"

The scientist switched off the current, and picked up a few metal objects from the platform that had fallen on to it during the operation: a ring, a watch, a propelling pencil, some coins and cuff-links. He put them in his pocket, stowed away the clothing half-reduced to dust in the cloakroom, and looked at me phlegmatically.

"I've just volatilized the Commissioner."

"But, damn it...!

We heard footsteps in the garden and opened the door. The aforementioned Beauléon presented himself, papers in hand. He scrutinized the room with his gaze and asked, with an astonished expression: "Where's Monsieur le Commissaire?"

"I don't know, my friend," said Pitoulet, quite calmly.

"Isn't he here, then?"

"Certainly not. He just left, a moment ago."

Beauléon went away.

Alone with Pitoulet, I resumed, in a voice blank with emotion: "What about Trypax?"

"Vanished. Beyond a certain voltage, the vaporous state becomes the gaseous state. Then the molecules dissociate. *Pfft!* And that's all. It's not important. A simple escape of gas!"

"*Escape of gas!* My word, that's rich! You've just killed a man."

"Me? Not at all. He's the one who wanted to take part in an experiment. He's had his experiment—absolute and total. Anyway, he was annoying me, that Trypax. He'd caused me too much trouble. So, *pfft!*"

Pitoulet was manifesting an increasing excitement I suddenly understood how that indiscreet young assistant he had told me about has disappeared. Another *pfft!*—and the assistant, an escape of gas...

I couldn't help shivering.

Beauléon suddenly reappeared, accompanied by a policeman, and asked again, in an anxious tone:

"Where's Monsieur le Commissaire? What have you done with Monsieur le Commissaire?"

Very annoyed at being mixed up in this business, I replied swiftly: "I don't know anything. I was in the garden, where I had to isolate myself, and I've just returned this instant."

"You, Monsieur Pitoulet—answer!"

"I repeat, Beauléon, that Monsieur le Commissaire disappeared without saying anything. Respectful of the police, I'm waiting for him."

The secretary and the policeman searched the laboratory. I trembled in case they opened the cloakroom. The idea never occurred to them. Then they explored the whole of the garden and the house, from top to bottom. Then they conferred, and departed rapidly, doubtless headed for the Commissariat.

Lifting up a curtain, we saw the little crowd of gossips dissipate, but we noticed that two policemen were continuing to guard the door.

XII. Anticipations

Now, of the two of us, it was Pitoulet who was displaying self-composure. Sitting in his study, he relaxed in a satisfied manner, with the aid of an open newspaper. I felt extremely ill-at-ease. When he started humming, I said to him: "You do realize that the affair might get worse?"

"Not for you, eh?" he said in a sarcastic tone. "You tried to save your own bacon. Don't worry: I won't drag you back into it."

I adopted a discontented and frosty expression. Then he threw himself into my arms, saying: "Forgive me, my dear Cabri. I know how devoted you are, how generous. You've given me more than enough proof. But I couldn't bear that Trypax. He was becoming impossible. Can you imagine that he had been martyrizing me for two hours before you arrived—that he had begun to ferret through my papers; that he was about to deliver into the public domain a series of secret and sublime formulae?"

"But in the final analysis, has he completely and definitively ceased to exist?"

"He has vanished into infinity, for all eternity."

"The police will come back. What will you tell them?"

"Still the same thing: that he left. It's the truth. The experiment hasn't left any trace. I'll throw what remains of his clothing in the fire, and melt the metallic objects I collected, in the electric furnace."

"Do you know, my dear Master, that you're terrifying?"

"Be philosophical, Cabri, my friend. Man is nothing but a shadow, the shadow of a shadow, as has just been demonstrated to you. I promise not to make that proof integrally. I'm placid—timid, even—but in front of the machine, the product of my genius. I recover my pride, my arrogance. When I saw Trypax on the platform, I thought I was seeing a scorpion on a page of Montaigne: I got rid of the matter that was soiling the mind. I made a man disappear; so be it. That doesn't prevent me from dedicating all my might to the happiness of humankind. I shall orient my discovery, which is replete with moral and practical applications, toward that sacred goal. I shall dedicate myself to finding a means of prolonging these temporary changes of state at will. I confess to you that the elastic state seems scarcely susceptible of useful applications—it's more a state of comical intermediacy—but the vaporous state, well disciplined, seems to offer the most beautiful promises, especially if it becomes possible to steer without difficulty in the opposite direction to an average wind.

"Firstly, what moral benefits! Knowing that it has become possible to penetrate everywhere, in the form of a shadow, to be observed without being aware of it, every one of us will elect to live, in his own home as well as in public, according to the rules of morality. All citizens will become sages, all inhabiting houses of glass.

"But most of all, what practical benefits! How easy and charming displacements and voyages will become! No fatigue in the course of the journey, no compression in carriages. A sensation of perpetual lightness. Then, on arrival, solidification. Anonymous societies will be founded, which will install transmutators at crossroads, in town squares and on the platforms of railway stations, much as one sees automatic vending-machines scattered around today.

"A complete transformation of means of communication will follow rapidly. I can easily imagine the vaporous traveler being introduced into a sort of pneumatic tube that will project him over the longest distances. I also foresee a revolution in therapeutics; it seems likely that the vaporous state will greatly facilitate the diagnosis and treatment of diseases; as for surgical interventions—child's play!

"It is nevertheless important, in my view, not to divulge the results of my discovery to anyone else, for the time being. Imagine how our information service and organization of combat would gain in marvelous flexibility, in matters of armed conflict. A vaporous officer would be able to cross enemy lines, spy on councils of war and bring back priceless information without difficulty. It would be possible, in matters of troop movement, to accumulate soldiers and horses within military trains in unlimited numbers. One would shrug one's shoulders on reading the old logistical advice—forty men, eight horses; forty thousand men, eight thousand horses—the latter would be easily accommodated, for they would be embarked in a vaporous state and solidified on disembarkation.

"If parallel experiments could eventually be realized in the vegetable and mineral kingdoms, there would then be an absolute upheaval in the conditions of terrestrial life: nebulous rocks, solid clouds, soft trees. Everything that exists on the globe would be at the mercy of the human will.

"Thus, little by little, climbing the steps of successive discoveries, Science penetrates Nature more fully, and a day will arrive when, finally lodged in the very bosom of Being, it will fuse with the Universe, will be the Universe's knowledge of itself, the Consciousness of the World!"

Swollen with pride and lyrical, Pitoulet prophesied—but while admiring him, I thought that it would be better for me not to be mixed up in his affairs from now on, and to go back to living in my lodgings in the Ternes. I cleverly took advantage of the pretext of my renewed engagement to plead that it was necessary for me to look after my appearance, and that all, because all my clothes and underwear were at home, I was obliged...

"You're not going to abandon me?" he asked, anxiously.

"How can you think so, my dear Master?" I protested, without being too sure whether I was sincere or not. "Too many bonds of friendship unite us—but I'm going to the theater this evening with the Bic family. I'll come back to see you tomorrow morning, and we'll have lunch together."

"Oh! Thank you"

I left him, not without relief, for I dreaded seeing the police arrive at any moment to arrest both of us. I foresaw grave complications, and had only one desire: to get out of there. Let those who have never been betrothed cast the first stone at me! How could I anticipate that the adventure was about to come apart in such a brutal and unexpected fashion?

XIII. Catastrophe and Marriage

At the door of the house I had to negotiate with the policemen on sentry duty, to whom I had to present my identity papers. When they were eventually satisfied that I was not Pitoulet and that I had a domicile, they let me go. I left calmly and unhurriedly, but when I turned the street corner I started running and jumping, happy to be free again, as if escaping from a nightmare.

I spent an exquisite evening at the Opéra-Comique, seated next to my Suzanne. *La Vie de Bohème* was playing.[25] My future parents-in-law, very moved by the sad fate of Mimi, accepted the celebration of our marriage in a fortnight's time. Intoxication!

"It appears, my boy," Bic said to me, "that you have left your chambers. Are you, then, renouncing a juridical career?"

"Not at all, my dear Monsieur," I replied, "but I've been working in the library for the last few days, in order to prepare my thesis."

"Really," said Bic, interestedly. "What is its subject, then?"

---

[25] *La Vie de Bohème* (1849) was the stage version of Henry Mürger's account of literary life in Paris prior to the 1848 Revoution, based on short stories written in 1846-49, which were expanded into an episodic novel in 1851 and became the basis for Puccini's opera *La Bohème* in 1896. The character of Mimi became the archetypal tragic *grisette*.

Ingeniously, I improvised. "Posthumous litigation in cases of emphyteusis."[26]

I promised myself firmly to return to the chambers the following morning, in order to distance myself completely from Pitoulet, who had become excessively compromising. Nevertheless, the following day, I judged it impossible that I should fail to keep my promise.

I went to the scientist's house. The door as still guarded. I reeled off my name and status, and obtained free access. I found the old inventor sitting in an armchair, with a doleful expression. He offered me a limp hand.

"What's up, my dear Master?"

"Alas, dear Cabri, what good did it do to yield to my impulse yesterday? For one Trypax lost, ten are found! Now it's that accursed Larigoule who's torturing me...who is even more terrible, in his own sly and insinuating fashion. I could resist Trypax with silence, but I sense that *to him*, I shall confess everything. Since your departure there has been nothing but juridical visits, investigations, supplementary and complementary enquiries...

"Then again, yesterday, I took care to burn the clothes, but I hid the little metal objects in a cupboard, counting on melting them down today. Now, seals have been put on that cupboard, and when it's opened again, they'll find Trypax's pencil, watch and cuff-links. I can't

---

[26] Emphyteusis is a kind of contract by which a heritable right of possession and use of land is ceded for a long period, or in perpetuity, on condition that the land is maintained in cultivation, or at least free from depreciation, and that an annual rent is paid.

explain that! Advise me, please! What can I do? I'm tempted to open the cupboard..."

I persuaded Pitoulet not to break the seals, severely prohibited by law, which would have also constituted a serious presumption of guilt.

"Oh!" he moaned, "if I could only get away! Still free in principle, however, I am, in fact, under surveillance. Yesterday, I wanted to go out. A policeman followed me, five paces behind. I had to turn back. My reputation is ruined. The entire neighborhood is convinced—so Gudule tells me—that I've buried Trypax in the garden. Me, an old man, him, that colossus! Are men more stupid than wicked, or more wicked than stupid? An insoluble enigma, that one!"

"But, my dear Master," I cried—for a luminous idea had just occurred to me, as so frequently happens—"in the face of serious danger, why not take a lesser risk? Go into the vaporous state! You can easily escape. The weather is fine, with not the slightest wind."

"Old fool!" he exclaimed. "You weren't thinking. Thank you, my young savior! Once solidified, I'll remain hidden long enough for it all to be forgotten. It's the very thing! Let's hasten to the laboratory!"

I had a strong feeling that I ought to leave him, but desire, and my sympathy for the unfortunate old man, impelled me to witness the experiment one last time. I followed him. He undressed, switched on the current, climbed up on to the platform, set the needle to "mist" and rotated the commutators.

The transformation began, and followed its course. As Pitoulet passed into the vaporous state, however I was astonished not to hear the usual bell. The electric clock must have broken down, for the current continued to flow.

I heard Pitoulet's voice: "Switch off the current, Cabri—switch it off!"

I shuddered as I realized that Pitoulet was at risk of Trypax's fate, and I bounded to the switches. In my haste, though—oh, when I think about it, I tear out my hair in remorse!—I must have made some kind of false move; one of the commutators stuck, and the current did not stop.

I saw Pitoulet's cloudy form become vaguer and vaguer. Panic-stricken, I ran to the console on the wall, found the necessary lever, and finally cut of the current.

Pitoulet had not completely dissipated, but what remained of him was less than a mist: a shadow of vapor which, having doubtless become lighter than air, suddenly rose upwards and flew away through an opening in the roof.

I ran into the garden, looking upwards—in vain. I could no longer see anything. What had become of him? Was he going to melt into the atmosphere, be diluted in the ether? Immediately or eventually? Temporarily or forever?

There was nothing more for me to do in the laboratory; I had, alas, already done too much. An idea crossed my mind and I smiled in spite of my grief. Perhaps, among the interstellar spaces, the imponderable residue of Pitoulet might meet up with the impalpable remains of Trypax. What extraordinary debates would unfold in infinity between those two dusty shadows! And I also thought that morality, so dear to Pitoulet, might, at the end of the day, find its settlement in that abrupt end: he had disappeared, a victim of the apparatus that had taken at least two human lives...

Almost consoled, I put on my hat and went out, proudly, already preparing my replies to the questions that the police were certainly going to ask me.

Indeed, the following day, the Commissioner of my district summoned me to his office and asked me to explain Pitoulet's disappearance. I could only tell him that I had talked to the old gentleman the day before, in the course of visiting him in my capacity as his legal advisor, that the policemen on sentry duty had seen me leave on my own, and that I knew no more. With regard to me, the affair ended there.

Pitoulet's mysterious disappearance was an event in the street, an incident in the quarter, and a banal news-item so far a public opinion was concerned. He left no heir. I feared momentarily that he might have made me his legatee, which would have attracted the undesirable attention of the police in my direction. The Great Transmutator, with its accessories, was sold off on behalf of the State and broken up for scrap, along with the rest of the deceased's possessions. The public was only represented by the usual auction crowd. Nevertheless, and elegant unknown came along to acquire a kind of dial on which two bizarre words were inscribed: *elastic* and *mist*.

The reader will have recognized my style in this delicate gesture. The dial is on my desk in Paris while I am writing these lines in X***, whose first edition I will dedicate to my tender Suzanne, now my wife. They will explain to her certain phenomena anterior to our union, whose interpretation I was unable to correct sooner, having been mobilized three days after my marriage.

Oh, if only Pitoulet's "Anticipations" had been realized, we would have known Victory much more rapidly! I also hope that my story will cure my delicate mother-in-law of her belief in spiritualism.

I understand as I finish, even better than when I started, how much incredulity this perfectly true story will encounter. I will permit myself to refer them to the official communiqués and related newspaper articles that situate the adventure, without any possible argument, within contemporary history.

For now, I have said all that I have to say, and I feel that my conscience is clear. It only remains for me to conclude with a solemn farewell to my admirable and ignored master, Jules-César-Guy Pitoulet, who, if he had not flown through the roof in the flower of his genius, would one day have revealed himself to the world as one of the Colonels of Science, one of the Caryatids of Humanity.

THE AGE OF LEAD

I. An Inconceivable Epidemic

It is irrefutable that the Gabon enjoys an elevated temperature, and it is no less certain that the days pass placidly there, exempt from the ridiculous trepidation of European life. Libreville, the colony's capital, is a delightful sea-port, with its picturesque aloe- and mangrove-wood huts, surrounded by gardens overflowing with abundant vegetation or dominated by cacti, lentisks, houseleeks and bocabungas. There are also sturdier edifices, built for the use of white men, but in the indigenous style; the bank is a beautiful building in pink brick, ornamented with genista bark, and the Lieutenant-Governor's palace a pretty tricolor house in peperino stone, aloe-wood branches and carob hearts.

Pasturelands extend around the city, which nourish numerous livestock—notably herds of buffalo whose steaks, braised with Congo onions, provide feasts for travelers. Eucalyptus and coconut woods punctuate the grasslands, where cockatoos, garden warblers and marmosets frolic.[27] Rattlesnakes and shrews swarm in the long grass.

---

[27] Falk's natural history is blithely askew; several of the species of the species he mentions in this chapter are not native to Central Africa. The most obvious sore thumbs are marmosets (*ouistitis* in French) and the capuchin monkey (*sapajou* in

The native villagers are gentle and cheerful by nature, shiny black in color; they are no more cannibals that the permanent secretary of the Académie Française. Everything in this blissful place seems, therefore, to respire the sweetness of life; and everything there was, indeed, respiring when, at 5:45 p.m. on March 21, 19--, a strange combination of circumstances contrived to disturb the legitimate quietude of M. Parmesif, the colony's Lieutenant-Governor.

Under the veranda with blue-paned bay windows, judiciously opening on to the cool shade of the garden, the Lieutenant-Governor and his faithful secretary, the elegant Monsieur Saumaître, both clad in white linen suits, were slowly drinking exquisite iced lemonade through straws. Between suctions, they were smoking odorous cigars, and whether they were sucking or puffing to the sway of their rocking-chairs, the mute and blissful gentlemen were not thinking about anything at all.

Their thought-free silence was suddenly torn apart by cries, sobs and an eruption of howls from Mademoiselle Lotte Parmesif, aged seven. The little girl was holding a bizarre package: a sort of ball of flaccid flesh, which she threw on to the table bearing the lemonade. The ball unwound; paws and a head emerged, and a frightful, unidentifiable little creature began bounding around the room. Meanwhile, Lotte curled up, weeping in her father's arms, and moaned: "Adolphe! Something's wrong with Adolphe, Papa!"

French), which are only found in South America, but his entire approach is cavalier.

The Lieutenant-Governor then recognized the bounding animal as young Adolphe, the child's pet capuchin monkey. "Catch him! Catch him, Saumaître!"

The elegant secretary bounded in pursuit of the minuscule quadrumane, and collected it from the wardrobe, using a monocle as bait. "Why, what's wrong with the monkey?" he asked in his turn, while the trembling animal rolled its frightened eyes.

"Something that's causing him to lose his hair," declared Parmesif—and he pulled out a few tufts that were still clinging to Adolphe's thigh, as easily as one removes the leaves from an overcooked artichoke. The capuchin monkey offered no resistance, nor did it cry; it did not seem to feel any pain; it limited itself to shivering, while stupidly clacking its jaws. Lotte began to cry again.

"Come on, calm down," her father said. "If Adolphe's ill, we'll look after him."

As he dried the child's tears, Madame Parmesif came in like a gust of wind. She was a handsome plump lady, with thick blonde hair and a little make-up on her eyebrows and a face, dressed in a jonquil kimono. She was followed by a mournful dog. She seemed very excited. "Gustave!" she said, violently. "Take a look at Top!"

Monsieur Parmesif observed that his wife's spaniel was losing its hair as copiously as his daughter's capuchin monkey.

"Yes," Madame Parmesif went on, "Top and Adolphe! Can you explain it?"

"Some kind of contagious alopecia," he suggested.

He had scarcely made this remark when an even strange phenomenon renewed his amazement. A bird had just fallen through an open window in the glazed ceiling; its wings could no longer sustain it, because it was very nearly de-feathered. Almost at the same time, Sokota, the Congolese servant, came on to the veranda; she was crying, and carrying a cage containing what was surely the most ridiculous parrot in the world.

Kiko had ceased to be the splendid multicolored macaw of the front steps; nothing more remained to him but a row of colored feathers on his head and rump—with the result that, with his round eyes, his brick-red skin, the row of feathers on his head and his guttural squawks, he resembled a grotesque and tiny caricature of a naked Redskin on the warpath.

Young Lotte howled even more loudly.

"Come on, Sokota!" said Monsieur Parmesif, impatiently. "Take the child away—we have to talk."

"The post, Monsieur le Lieutenant-Gouverneur."

"Thanks, Saumaître…why…well…that's odd! And this letter too…and this….read this, Saumaître…"

The handsome Madame Parmesif and the impeccable Saumaître seized the papers that the Lieutenant-Governor's feverish hand was holding out to them, and it was their turn to utter an arpeggio of exclamations.

This resulted from the correspondence from Libreville and its surroundings, which revealed that all the animals on the land and in the air were losing their fur and feathers, at variable speeds but to a similar degree—that of total deprivation. For no apparent reason, the cattle, sheep, horses, dogs, cats, pigs and rabbits on the farms, all the poultry in the chicken-runs, the animals living in luxury in the houses and the wild animals in the woods, were being visibly transformed into supernudities—if one might put it thus—as wretched as they were baroque.

With his thumb on his forehead, Parmesif reflected. Violently, he cried: "Good God! What's all this about? A veritable conspiracy of beasts. Here, where we're so tranquil! We must mount an investigation, demand reports, and produce them. What do you think of this business, Saumaître?

The perfect secretary replied, deferentially: "It seems to require attention."

"Come in!" shouted Parmesif.

A black manservant came in, with several telegrams in his hand. The Lieutenant-Governor opened them anxiously. He read aloud:

"From Najalé: *Maritime Commissioner to Lieutenant-Governor. Conspicuous rain of bird feathers on coast. Please telephone instructions.*

"From the Administration at Nyanga: *Administrative livestock herds victim general alopecia. Please send official veterinarian urgently.*

"From Mayouniba: *Rubber plantations in danger. General shriveling of district vegetation. Awaiting orders.*

"From Lastourville: *Epidemic in park. Ostriches de-plumed. Telegraph advice.*

"And from the plantations of Franceville: *Banana-trees suffering. Coconut-palms dying. Send help urgently.*"

The pale Madame Parmesif said: "The coconut-palms? The banana-trees? Oh!"

"Yes," said her husband, whose face was crimson. "The plants are joining in now. Damn it, Saumaître, what does it all mean?"

"I don't know, sir."

Behind the door, however, loud voices were raised. Two black men were arguing bitterly.

"No see Massa Tenant-gov'nor!" declare the butler.

"Me haf talk him urgent!" protested another voice, which Parmesif recognized as that of one of his old farmers."

A white-haired native came in, with his peaked straw hat in his hands. He was dressed up, wearing a blue jacket, khaki trousers, and a red cretonne cravat; yellow gloves compensated for the grey nudity of his feet. There was a shiny watch-chain in his waistcoat, but no watch. Without any preamble, he began: "Mass gov'nor, you cattle is losing dey skin."

"Their skin? Jibber-jabber! Their hair, you mean?"

"No, no. Dey hair already gone. Now dey skin is fallin…like dis." And the old man demonstrated by detaching a long strip of epidermis from his arm.

"Oh! What! Saumaître, telephone Monsieur Réminiscent—tell him to come and see me immediately."

"Very well."

While his secretary strode stiffly to the telephone, Parmesif set his elbows on the balcony of the veranda. He could see his daughter and her companion immobile in the garden, contemplating the ground as if petrified. Their attitude alarmed him, but his alarm increased while he mechanically directed a circular glance outside.

He called his wife. "Come and look at this, dear!"

Madame Parmesif hurried to his side.

"Look at the trees," he continued. "Look! Our beautiful magnolia: don't the leaves seem to you to have dried up, as if they'd been burned?"

"Yes," she said, in a choked voice. "Neither its leaves, not those of the other trees, have their natural tint any longer. One might think that they were dying, that they were shriveling up fatally. Oh, my dear, extraordinary things are happening around us. And what's the matter with Lotte and Sokota?"

She called to her daughter. The child raised her head and threw herself upon the bosom of the old black woman, tearfully. She was clutching a handful of dry grass. Very anxiously, Madame Parmesif said: "Come here right away!"

They hurried over, and little Lotte, her face flooded with tears, held out a bunch of yellowed flowers to her mother.

"Look what's become of them, Mama!"

Indeed, the flowers, which had been alive, colorful and odorous a day earlier—even an hour earlier—were no longer anything but specters of their former selves, devoid of brightness or perfume.

"Is like dat ever'where, de flow," said Sokota. "Is all sick, gwin to die."

"Gustave, Gustave—I'm frightened!"

Parmesif gestured to his wife to shut up, for their daughter was looking at them in terror. He promised the child a large coconut, and she left, consoled. Left alone with Madame Parmesif, he said: "Do you want to drive the child out of her mind?"

"I'm terrified myself," she replied.

In an agitated voice, he went on: "Calm down. All these fantastic phenomena must have a causal explanation. Anyway, here's the vet."

II. Réminiscent's Diagnosis

The official veterinarian, Monsieur Réminiscent, arrived at a trot, sweating and out of breath. He was the Lieutenant-Governor's neighbor, and while bending down to kiss Madame Parmesif's sadly-extended hand, he explained that he had escaped between two consultations. He was a short stout man with a black goatee and a ruddy and acne-ridden complexion, obviously a drinker. A fan woven from little wrinkles spread out from each of his little eyes; he rolled his *r*s as if he were pulverizing bricks.

"Excuse me," he said, "for only staying a moment. My office has been invaded. Apart from my assistant, my wife and my three daughters, I have my niece, Aunt Anaïs and the son of the fruiterer who works in my office pounding pomades and mixing distempers..."

"Well, in a word, Monsieur Réminiscent, can you explain to us...are we dealing with an epidemic?"

"Not exactly—an epizootic disease."

"All right. Do you know that it extends much further than you think? I have reports, letters and telegrams here; it's affecting almost the whole colony."

"No!"

"It's therefore necessary to take immediate measures—but in order to take them, we need to know the cause..."

"I've found it."

"Oh, do tell us!" begged Madame Parmesif.

"Well, here it is: the skin of the infected animals is falling off in strips and sheets; it's a progressive desquamation, in consequence of a sort of molting."

"What?"

"Well, we're in serpent territory. Large and small, they're abundant in the country, and even in the city. No longer ago than yesterday, I found a grass snake asleep on my doormat. Now, we're in the season when snakes shed their skin; that molting has become contagious, that's all."

A silence veiled by amazement greeted this revelation. The audience reflected. Monsieur Saumaître, with a great deal of courteous reverence, objected: "It would be the first time…"

"Perhaps—but in matters of science, it's necessary not to despair of anything. This epizootic disease leads me to infer that molting, in snakes, is microbial in origin—and the molt microbe has just turned noxious. Some animals must have consumed shreds of snakeskin left in corners. They've molted in their turn. Others have eaten their skin—or even absorbed contaminated pellicles without eating them, via the dust in the air or in some other way.

"You're not unaware that, for example, scarlet fever is contagious in humans during the season of desquamation. The molt is evidently an analogous sort of fever, for it's accompanied in animals, to begin with, by an elevation of temperature and a congestion of the pharynx. It only remains to identify the molt microbe, for which I have already reserved a name: *Bacillus reminiscens*. Now, this infinitely small organism has revealed itself to be all the more virulent in taking effect for the first time. That's the cause of the lightning spread of the epizootic condition. I've made up lotions and unguents: makeshift therapies. What we need is a serum, then a prophylactic vaccine. We shall find them. It's an important matter."

And he clicked his heels joyfully.

"But what about the birds?" said Madame Parmesif.

"Birds scavenge, pecking the ground. Besides, don't forget that some birds also molt."

"They lose their feathers, not their skin!"

"A difference of degree, a question of more or less. Here's something that will convince you. I've made use of the experimental method, highly recommended in science. I took two canaries; to one, I gave snakeskin, via the beak; to the other, nothing. The experimental canary lost its feathers and its skin twice as fast as the control canary. It's peremptory. Have you any sick animals here?"

"First of all, there's poor Top here," sighed Madame Parmesif. "Look, he's almost hairless…"

"Indeed. It's not pretty. And his skin is starting to come away too. Perfect. Same treatment as the comrades: applications of my lotion, *reminiscine*. For the larger animals, Monsieur le Gouverneur, use a brush to wash them with *reminiscol*, my liniment. You can obtain these products from me."

"No internal remedy?"

"A little later, a few good purges, Monsieur le Gouverneur. Would you excuse me, Madame? I have to attend to my fellow citizens."

"Just a moment. What about the plants? How do you explain their withering?"

"That's not within my competence—you'll have to ask a botanist. Personally, I think it might be due to the depredations of an insect analogous to *Phylloxera*, which I'm not qualified to discover. On which note…"

He bade farewell.

"Shall we have the pleasure of seeing you this evening?" asked Madame Parmesif.

"I shall try to escape briefly, my dear Madame. No one has been talking about anything but your reception for a week. I shall try to put in an appearance."

"Alas," she said, plaintively, "I fear that these events do not bode well."

"So far as I'm concerned, I don't deplore them," the veterinarian replied. "Be tranquil, dear Madame. Your *soirée* will be brilliant."

The general opinion, after his departure, was that Monsieur Réminiscent was becoming unbearable, but that one had to smile at him, since he had suddenly become the arbiter of destiny in Libreville and its surrounds.

III. The Governor's Soirée

As night fell, however, even more serious news pushed public concern with the mysterious malady of plants and animals into the background, for the epidemic had taken a further leap: it had begun to attack human beings—colored people, fortunately. A number of natives had suddenly begun to lose their skin, and there was a discordant concert of groans throughout the city. In response to entreaties, the sorcerers were selling strong liquor and organizing sacred dances, for whose favorable effects the participants waited in vain. That evening, therefore, when the elite of Librevillean society met at the Lieutenant-Governor's house, the only subject of conversation was the dread of seeing the malady afflict white people and suddenly experiencing, at ten o'clock or thereabouts, the terror of knowing that the white race had been contaminated in its turn.

In fact, while the guests savored iced syrups in the delightfully starry night, listening to the tenor Caruso in phonographic form, the police captain—who was twirling his moustache while flirting with the postmaster's wife—had a feeling that the moustache in question had come away in his hand. It had—and that distinguished officer was not the only victim of such a sinister accident. In the course of that memorable soirée, the epidermis of every guests began to denude itself, to varying degrees but appreciable in every case.

Monsieur Pitourin-Mocquard, the president of the Court, who was talking about literature with Madame Parmesif, suddenly found that a tuft of his beautiful beard had become detached from his chin, and was scattered over his waistcoat and trousers. As for Madame Parmesif, while trying to extract a hairpin from the edifice of her coiffure, she also pulled away, without the slightest difficulty, a handful of her golden hair. Some people lost their eyelashes, others an eyebrow or two, others their bodily hair—and everyone realized that it hardly mattered where the malady first exhibited itself in any individual case; experiment proved that the enigmatic alopecia was rapidly becoming total.

It seemed certain that the loss of hair would be succeeded by a period of desquamation. This lamentable prospect distressed the most highly-placed hearts. Only Monsieur Parmesif, habitually clean-shaven and already bald, conserved his self-composure, as befit a leader of men. He calmly interrogated, not the veterinarian—who had abruptly become a dull nonentity—but Dr. Columat, the city's leading physician.

Amid a group of listeners hanging on to his every word, the latter replied: "I don't understand it at all. This story of contagion from the molting of snakes is, of course, utterly grotesque. I'm inclined to think that we're the victims of a virulent dermatosis, probably of parasitic origin. Is it a kind of leprosy? Is it a blood-infection? Is it the effect of a trypanosome? Is it…?"

He was interrupted by one of his listeners, a retired ship's captain and a distinguished naturalist. "Excuse me, Doctor, but one fact ought to be noted whose omission might corrupt any hypothesis. Concurrently with ours, a contagious infection is corroding plants, producing parallel effects. The light of these electric lamps is sufficient to show us the ravages produced: the leaves on the trees are curling up, as if burnt; those fleshy plants, hitherto so plump, are flattened, as if emptied out; these flowers, blooming vividly yesterday, are now faded and sickly, and will be dead tomorrow. Why?"

This interruption only served to increase the general anxiety. Everyone now sensed that a single unknown and deadly influence was extending over both kingdoms of nature throughout the Gabon.

"And what do you conclude, Monsieur?" the physician asked the naturalist.

"I conclude, Doctor, that this is not a matter of parasitic manifestation—and the hypothesis I offer far surpasses yours in amplitude. I suspect that the air of the Gabon is presently subject to a chemical modification—that the atmosphere in which we are all plunged contains some unknown new gas which, without destroying life itself, is harmful to living tissues. In my opinion, we should not even be talking about contagion. If a storm bursts and we are all wet, does that mean that rain is contagious? Oh, my God…!"

While speaking, the naturalist had been rubbing his cheeks rather vigorously, and that gesture had just ripped away one of his fine side-whiskers.

"Hair today," he said, sadly, "tomorrow the epidermis, the dermis the day after. It could be that within a week, this corrosive gas will make us all, beasts and humans alike, into pitiful flayed creatures."

A woman fainted. The reception ended with lugubrious farewells.

Once he was alone with his secretary, the Governor declared: "We must telegraph the Ministry."

The composition of an explicit dispatch kept them up all night.

IV. The Peeled Equator

The next day the citizens abroad in Libreville only recognized one another with the greatest difficulty. To avoid the scarcely-attractive appearance of partial depilation, men had shaved off their beards and moustaches. It was as if an army of actors had taken possession of the city, to the exclusion of all other inhabitants. Alone in the midst of public distress, the wigmakers were walking on air. They could not meet demand, and became insolent—which, for the favored individuals, save for a few honorable exceptions, constituted the greatest satisfaction in the world.

At 10 a.m., Monsieur Parmesif was still asleep, worn out by fatigue. All night long, he had been subjected to the lamentations of his wife, who was already half-bald; young Lotte, in her turn, was losing her golden curls, her parents' silken pride and joy. When the Governor had negligently opened his eyes, however, and run them—distractedly at first, then with fascination—over a telegram from the Minister, he leapt out of bed, got dressed and raced to the office, where Monsieur Saumaître was waiting for him, as hairless and shiny as an egg.

"Read this!" cried Parmesif.

And Monsieur Saumaître read:

Same phenomena observed in Congo, English East Africa, Singapore, Borneo, Brazil. Colombia. International investigation begun. Cause of epidemic still unknown. Keep population calm. Will telegraph instructions as soon as possible.

The two men looked at one another in amazement.

"In that case," Parmesif exclaimed, spinning a little terrestrial globe, "it's the entire equator that's peeling!"

After reflection, Monsieur Saumaître replied: "The entire equator is, indeed, peeling."

They sank into meditation. They visualized the Earth, effectively girdled around its zero degree of latitude by peoples of the most disparate sorts, but equally terrified by the common peril. At the same time, they estimated that, if the doctor's hypothesis was false, the naturalist's was insufficient, for it seemed impossible to them that the terrestrial atmosphere should be contaminated uniquely around the perimeter corresponding to the globe's greatest circumference. Why there? Why not elsewhere?

Other distressing news reached them; vessels that had been sailing for several days in the vicinity of the equator were reaching port with their crew and passengers losing their skins; it seemed that their maritime voyage had accentuated the effects of the mysterious malady. In some voyagers, the skin was crumbling into dust, in others it was coming away in shreds. Their despair appeared to be attenuated when they learned that the same disease was ravaging land-dwellers—and it really was a matter of ravaging now, for the epidemic, whose initial effects had seemed more ridiculous than dangerous, soon took on a manifest character of gravity.

Some people fell victim to intense nervous afflictions; many field-workers were subject to a weakening of their sight, and to lesions in the eye that were sometimes manifest as cataracts. In many cases, the spleen seemed to be affected; it diminished in volume and became spongy. Phenomena of rapid consumption were observed in children. Many of them displayed profound lesions in the skin comparable to burns, painless but destructive of the tissues.

As for the vegetation, it was reminiscent of an autumn in Tibet after a hot summer: the reddened foliage of the trees hung down miserably, or was strewn funereally over the ground. It seemed that the universal malady was enveloping the peeling equator like a devouring sash, some vast cousin of the shirt of Nessus—and an intolerable anguish consumed all the inhabitants of the globe's torrid region.

V. The Scourge Spreads

For the Equator, the initial seat of the epidemic, already only constituted a minor part of the contaminated regions. The scourge was not only gaining in vigor but also in extent, and its stain was spreading implacably toward the temperate zones of both hemispheres.

A month after its appearance, the "universal leprosy" encircled the entire ring extended between the Tropic of Cancer and the Tropic of Capricorn—and it was no longer mere lieutenant-governors and colonial officials who were agitatedly reporting by telegram to the metropolitan authorities; now it was the Metropolises themselves, the great civilized States of the planet's temperate zones, that were exchanging urgent messages.

The army of scientists was mobilized. This time, it was up to them, and them alone, to save human existence, if that were possible. That army, however, was not composed entirely of generals, and the collision of hypotheses only generated discussion, and no light. The enigma, it is true, was becoming more complicated, for the scourge was now exercising its influence excessively on inanimate objects. Thus, it had become impossible in the affected regions to take photographs; all plates and films, freshly taken out of their boxes, were found to be clouded in advance of their exposure to daylight. It was also impossible to make wireless telegraphy apparatus work—during the day, at least, for communication was reestablished at night. Why?

It was these particular perturbations, even more inexplicable than the others in the minds of the multitude, that drew the researches of the scientists in a new direction. By this time, Mexico, the United States, Morocco, Algeria, Arabia, Egypt, Persia, Hindustan and Tonkin— which is to say, all the countries in the Northern Hemisphere within the 30th degree of latitude—and the corresponding regions in the Southern Hemisphere, were prey to the scourge, whose violence was increasing every day.

In the equatorial regions deaths were multiplying, and the appearance of men and animals at the moment of death was as follows: epidermis completely hairless; skin ulcerated in the regions of the body most hidden from the Sun; intense conjunctivitis; blepharitis and cataracts. The cutaneous wounds did not manifest any tendency to heal.

Thus, on the one hand there was a progressive and continuous burning of organic tissues; on the other, a cessation by night of certain magnetic perturbations. The conclusion drawn from this assembly of facts by several scientific conferences was that the initial cause of the scourge must be attributed to the source of all heat and all light: the Sun.

It became, in fact, increasingly probable that some specific solar activity had entered into play—but what? The telescopes of all the observatories in the world were aimed at the star. Nothing abnormal was observed. It seemed to the astronomers of Paris and Uppsala that the sunspots, generally dark red in color, were turning blood-red—but they had not changed in their form, their number or their extent. Besides, their influence on the seasons, and particularly on the terrestrial temperature, was still debatable. The Academies, in public sessions, whose conclusions were distributed in official communiqués, declared that sunspots could not be causing any disease of the skin or of the cuticles of plants.

Meanwhile, the scourge continued its methodical and ineluctable progress.

VI. Monsieur Galfo

Now, it seemed to have been determined by destiny that Monsieur Parmesif, a tiny particle of humanity, would play an important role in this adventure of universal interest, either individually or in terms of his family. Abandoning the affairs to the colony to the hands of Monsieur Saumaître for a few weeks, on the Minister's authority, he followed the example of all the people in the affected regions who were able to move. He took his wife and daughter north, specifically to Neuilly-sur-Seine, the town of his birth, where he owned a small house.

France was still unaffected, but the minds of her people—like all others at similar latitudes—were singularly overexcited. Parmesif, who announced his imminent return to the Gabon among the circle of his acquaintances, was unanimously admired. The Minister promised him the Croix d'Officier de la Légion d'Honneur and as Saumaître was, after all, entirely competent, Parmesif decided to wait for a decrease in the epidemic before going back to Libreville. He followed the newspaper reports of the daily progress of the scourge with a sort of avid horror.

One afternoon, he was scanning the "latest" edition of the *Bonsoir* when he read:

One of our eminent young scientists, M. Stéphane Galfo, has today delivered a report on the scourge to the Académie des Sciences. The document remains secret, but a highly qualified authority has been able to assure us that it reveals the cause—and, in consequence, the remedy—of the "universal leprosy". The world will learn important things tomorrow.

The other evening newspapers carried near-identical articles.

"Galfo!" he said to his wife. "Isn't that...?"

"Yes!" she exclaimed. "Stéphane Galfo is one of my cousins—Uncle Victor's son. We were once very close..."

"Where does he live?"

"Wait a minute..."

Madame Parmesif went into her bedroom. She came back with a little address-book and found her husband with his hat already on his head. "If he hasn't moved," she said, "his address is 17A, Rue Herschel."

Parmesif bounded into the Avenue de Neuilly, and then into an automobile.

Galfo had not moved. Having rung three times on the threshold of the fourth-floor apartment occupied by his cousin by marriage, however, Parmesif received the response, from a burly and arrogant maid, that Monsieur Galfo was not seeing anyone. "You're not the first to come today, and you certainly won't be the last!"

Indeed, a gentleman who had just climbed the stairs stopped on the landing and asked for Monsieur Galfo.

The maid replied to both visitors: "No one. Monsieur is seeing absolutely no one; he's given orders."

"I beg your pardon," said Parmesif. "Here's my card. I'm his cousin, temporarily in Paris. I've come from the Gabon for urgent consultation. His cousin, be sure to tell him..."

The maid took Parmesif's card, with an expression of disgust and closed the door again. "I don't think," the latter said to the other visitor "that you have any chance of getting in."

"Yes I do, Monsieur—I'm the representative of an important scientific journal."

"Nothing to do with us," Parmesif declared. "Ah! Now we'll see!"

The door had opened again. Come in, you," the maid said to him.

"Madame, I…" said the representative.

"No, not you!" And she slammed the door violently.

"It's unfortunate," Parmesif pronounced, "that one can't be left alone in one's own home. Where is my dear cousin?"

The chambermaid introduced him into a small scantily-furnished drawing-room. "Wait," she said, and went out.

Parmesif sat down in an old green plush armchair. Shortly afterwards, he saw a thin, pale fellow of about thirty come in. The newcomer had a long beard and a soft smile; the gaze of blue eyes seemed very refined and benevolent.

Parmesif threw himself into the young man's arms. "Galfo! My dear cousin!" He recounted, very rapidly, the story of his arrival in Paris with his family, and went on: "I'll get straight to the point. Later, I hope, you will fill me in about your life and work. I know that you're a scientist…"

"Since yesterday evening," said Galfo, smiling.

"Right! I'm no better informed than I am. My wife, your cousin, is desperate—bald, my dear friend, absolutely bald—and my daughter is also very ill. Is it really true that you have made a discovery?"

"Yes—yesterday. My report has been in the hands of the Dean of the Faculty of Sciences for a few hours. It will be made public tomorrow."

"Then tell me, quickly—what is the cause of the scourge?"

"My dear cousin," Galfo replied, calmly, "I cannot, in deference to the Dean, who has accepted my report, reveal any of my observations."

"Even to me—to me your cousin…?"

"My cousin is only one man. Besides, the peril will not have increased greatly in one more day. Nevertheless, informally, I recommend that you…"

VII. J. S. Barcklett

He interrupted himself. A noise of loud voices was resonating in the antechamber. The maid was shouting: "Nothing doing, I tell you! He's not seeing anyone."

A sonorous foreign accent replied: "But I want to see him. I have to!"

The maid began to shouted even louder, but abruptly fell silent. A moment later, she presented herself, rather shamefacedly. "This gentleman," she said "insisted so strongly...he's come from America."

"Whether from America or Asnières, I don't want to see anyone," he said, with gentle firmness.

Meanwhile, Parmesif had glanced at the card and read:

J. S. BARCKLETT
Philadelphia
U.S.A.

Galfo continued: "Some machine salesman—Americans are great producers."

Parmesif, who was thinking hard, cried: "I have it! Barcklett of Philadelphia! Either I'm much mistaken, or he's a multimillionaire."

"Definitely!" said the chambermaid—after which she bit her lip.

"I've seen his photograph," Parmesif continued. "I'll recognize him. Let him in, my boy—you've nothing to lose."

"All right," said Galfo.

When the maid had gone out, Parmesif added: "If Barcklett's put himself out, old chap, it's because it's an important business matter. He's a big financier, one of the richest owners in the Klondike…"

At that moment, a broad-shouldered individual with a round head, a ruddy face and a carefully-shaped moustache dressed in a suit the color of tobacco made a rapid entrance.

"That's him!" Parmesif murmured to Galfo.

The American had not come in alone, though: he was followed by a young woman, whose beauty, complexion and slimness were ideal. She was clad in a white muslin dress, slightly off-the-shoulder, which displayed the nape of her gracious neck. Her cheerful smile, revealing dazzling teeth, lit up the little room.

The foreigner, his palm open, hesitated between the two men. "Monsieur Galfo?" In response to a movement from the scientist, he went on: "Delighted. J. S. Barcklett of Philadelphia here, and his daughter Winnie."

She smiled, archangelically. "Bonjour, Monsieur," she said, extended a slender and vigorous hand to the blushing Galfo.

"Introduce me," whispered Parmesif.

"Oh, sorry! My cousin, Gustave Parmesif, Lieutenant-Governor of the Gabon."

Parmesif bowed formally. Barcklett shook his hand, and continued, in incorrect but comprehensible French: "If you will permit, let's sit down. I'll explain why I'm here. My daughter and I have come for a short stay in Paris. Winnie is very interested in your literature, and I introduced myself this morning to the secretariat of the Faculty, in order to enroll her in Professor Poule's course on your Baudelaire…"

"Oh, I'm so fond of Baudelaire!" sighed the young woman, raising eyes like green lakes toward the ceiling.

"Then we took a walk through the Sorbonne, admiring the paintings and colored frescos. We passed in that manner from the Faculty of Letters to that of Sciences. There, on a staircase, I saw two lavishly decorated gentlemen talking animatedly. While examining a bas-relief, I lent an ear. One, who had long grey hair and a hooked chin…"

"The Dean," said Galfo.

"…was saying to the other, who had two noses—or rather, one nose with a double bump…"

"I know who you mean. Then…"

"…he said to him: 'This Galfo's report will produce a thunderbolt.' Yes, he said thunderbolt. And the other added: 'What a rush there'll be tomorrow…' They drew away. I didn't hear any more—but I remembered the name: Galfo. At the secretariat of the Faulty, I learned that you had a laboratory…"

"Of radiophysics, to be exact."

"But neither at the secretariat nor at your laboratory, which was locked, could I obtain your private address."

"Orders have been given to that effect."

"Well, I got your address all the same, like everything else I want—and here I am. Since there'll be a rush, there must be a product. You give me the name of the product right away, and this evening, I'll send out all the possible instructions. Tomorrow, I'll be the owner of large quantities, and tomorrow, at the same time. You'll get your hands on a check at the America Eagle, the amount of which I'm waiting for you to name."

While speaking, he fetched a checkbook and a pen out of his pocket.

Galfo remained nonplussed. Parmesif assumed an advantageous pose.

"What sum, Monsieur?" Barcklett repeated, his pen raised.

"Monsieur," Galfo replied, blushing again, "I'm not a businessman but a man of science. I can't sell you the name or the formula of a remedy, the knowledge of which will necessarily be entailed by that of the cause of the scourge. There will be nothing—absolutely noth-ing—secret, and in consequence, I do not consider that I have the right to sell you anything."

As he said this, Galfo received a jab in his side from Parmesif's elbow.

Winnie took up the thread: "Monsieur Galfo, what you say is very nice, and very French, but you must do as I ask. You're going to give my Papa the name of the remedy immediately, and I will write something on the check myself, which Papa will sign. There you are!" She matched words with action, held out the checkbook to her father, and placed the check on the table.

"No," Galfo protested, "that's not necessary." And, revealing what he would doubtless have kept quiet if Barcklett had come alone, he declared: "The remedy is lead."

"Lead?"

"Yes, Monsieur. I'll explain…"

"Don't bother. I don't have a minute to lose before giving my instructions. I'll buy all the lead available immediately. Winnie?"

"Papa?"

"Are you coming, child? You need to buy an entire library for Professor Poule's course."

"No, Papa. I've changed my mind. Poetry no longer interests me. I want to study radiophysics—with Monsieur Galfo, if he's agreeable…"

"If I'm agreeable! Oh, Mademoiselle!"

"When will you show me your laboratory? Tomorrow?"

"Of course, Mademoiselle—tomorrow."

Galfo stared for a long time at the door through which Winnie Barcklett had disappeared from view.

Meanwhile, Parmesif examined the check. "$5000," he said. "That's nice—which doesn't alter my opinion that you've been swindled. You should have obtained a contract of partnership with a share of the profits. Now, will you explain to me?"

"Tomorrow…" Murmured Galfo, as if transported by a dream.

And Parmesif could not dissipate his cousin's dreaminess.

VIII. A Sensational Report

In any case, his curiosity was satisfied—along with that of the entire world—the following morning. The newspapers had never appeared with such gigantic headlines:

UNIVERSAL ALOPECIA VANQUISHED.
ITS CONQUEROR STÉPHANE GALFO.

VICTORY OF FRENCH SCIENCE:
YOUNG SCIENTIST DEFEATS THE SCOURGE

MIND TRIUMPHS OVER MATTER
THANKS TO STÉPHANE GALFO'S DISCOVERY

There followed various paeans in praise of the master, in the Pindaric mode. Most of the papers also took it upon themselves to explain the discovery either by summarizing or by paraphrasing his report, in consequence offering murky enlightenment. Some more wisely limited themselves to reproducing the text. It was conceived as follows:

Monsieur le Doyen,
About a month ago, I was able to observe certain inexplicable perturbations in the functioning of the exceedingly sensitive apparatus comprising the radiophysics laboratory that you were kind enough to allocate to me.

At intervals that were initially widely spaced, but then became closer, they were abruptly deprived of their electric charges, with no apparent cause.

I became greatly troubled when, in the course of spectrographic research, I noticed the appearance of new lines in the solar spectrum—lines quite distinct from those studied by Frauenhofer and so completely mapped by Angström.

That fact put me on the track. Having charged an electroscope, I directed a ray of sunlight upon it I saw the gold leaf fall back almost immediately to the zero point of the scale. My conclusion was, therefore, that solar radioactivity had suddenly increased, in such a proportion that the effects would be manifest both rapidly and violently.

But why had the scourge begun to produce its effects at the Equator, which then extended toward the Poles? Evidently, because the Sun's ray fall vertically at the Equator, the increase in radioactivity was manifested more quickly there; as distances from the Equator increase, the rays fall more obliquely, by virtue of the well-known "cosine law," and are therefore less powerful. That is why the phenomenon, which, in reality commenced everywhere at the same time, appeared to spread from the Equator to the Poles. As for its effects, they are those, immensely amplified, of a source of "gamma rays."

It is known that among physical agents, these rays are in the first rank as regards their harmfulness; not content with acting at the surface, like heat, light and ultra-violet radiation, they act internally, by virtue of their property of traversing the various tissues of an organism to a greater or lesser depth. They have a pernicious effect on all living cells, especially the cells of cer-

tain particular organs, which are the genital organs, nerve-ganglions, white corpuscles and the skin. In brief, even at low doses, they provoke a premature senescence of all living cells—and, if the dose is sufficient, their definitive death.

Now, all the observed phenomena are evidently identical with those determined by gamma radiation. Not being a doctor of medicine, I will not enter into detail regarding the syndromes whose pathology I have only sketched out.

How can the peril be averted? The gravity of past, present and future accidents necessitates the creation, with the briefest possible delay, of all the known means of protection against solar radioactivity.

In the present state of our knowledge, there is one product, and one alone, that is completely opaque to gamma radiation: lead, whether isolated or in combination, in glass or crystal, canvas or rubber. In this regard, radiologists have shown us the way: they possess sufficiently complete protective apparatus. The defense of the hands, as is well-known, is achieved by means of leaded rubber gloves, that of the eyes by leaded glass spectacles, that of the body by aprons made out of leaded cloth. In our case, however, the dangerous radiations do not emerge from a source that can be channeled; they surround the interested parties in all directions, and there will have to be a considerable practical adaptation of existence to these new conditions—if, at least, as seems probable, humankind desires to continue to exist.

This is not the place to imagine the protective devices that will doubtless see the light of day in countless varieties. My purpose was merely to specify the origin of the scourge, thus to indicate the remedy.

It will be as well to utilize the devices in question as quickly as possible, for there can be no further doubt, at present, that the gamma rays have already begun their silent ravages upon the organisms of this country. I estimate that, if no precautions are taken, we shall have the first serious incidents to deplore within the next fortnight.

IX. The Run on Lead

Equity demands that it be noted that other radiologists had carried out analogous experiments at the same time as Monsieur Galfo, leading to identical conclusions, but they had formulated them less rapidly. The young scientist's priority being established, therefore, the new rays emitted by the Sun were named "Galfo rays." That was incontestably a source of illustration for the scientific hero, but no profit derived from it for him, nor to those to whom the scourge had, thus far, delivered honest benefits. Within a few hours, all the physicians, including the most specialized lost their entire clientele; pharmacists lamented beside their immense neglected stocks of lotions, depuratives and philodermic unguents. If Galfo's observations had not been irrefutable, several trades unions would have launched furious lawsuits against him. No one, however, undertook any such economic action, for they were prey to more pressing worries; it was, in effect, a matter of everyone procuring, without delay, the quantity of lead necessary to protect his life.

On the day when the panacea was revealed, the scourge had reached the 44th degree of latitude—which represented, for France, a line drawn almost directly between Morcenx and Puget-Théniers. In consequence, Toulouse was peeling, as were Mont-de-Marsan, Albi, Avignon and Nîmes. The run on lead therefore began, with lightning rapidity. "Run on lead" is not sufficiently precise; on the part of the masses, there was a race for available lead susceptible of furnishing the desired protection; and on the part of businessmen there was a run on the metal itself. In the space of a few hours, therefore, the run on lead reached vertiginous heights—heights all the more fantastic because the mineral deposits happened to be on the property of a few individuals and societies, which regulated the extraction of the primary material at their convenience. Thanks to the advantage he had over his peers, Barcklett was the largest owner of the precious metal, the Lead King.

In France, mines of cerussite and galena, the carbonates and sulphates from which lead is extracted, are situated in Brittany and Auvergne. In the short time available, Barcklett had only been able to purchase four—but he possessed one of them in America, where lead ores are rare. Above all, however, he was assured of the definite sale of the entire disposable production of his factories. In league with a few rich financiers, he soon achieved dominion over the run.

Before the crisis, the average price of lead had been about forty centimes a kilogram; within 48 hours it passed three francs. Undoubtedly, the trust-owners would have been able to let it go higher still, but they rightly feared the intervention of governmental powers in a matter of general concern.

For their part, the factory-owners formed cartels; in very little time, certain wholesalers built up enormous fortunes. All the installations that could be adapted to the metallurgy of lead were dedicated to that work, and a few days sufficed to modify the economics of human life completely.

X. The Age of Lead

It was individual initiative that first came into play. Every individual exerted his ingenuity to obtain effective protection for himself. All the sheets of lead that producers and merchants possessed were bought up, and the buyers remained huddled in their houses or sitting under sheets of lead all day long. These fortunate individuals were, inevitably, a tiny minority.

On the advice of the Académie of Sciences, urgently convened, the Government put up posters advising citizens to spend the day, as far as possible, in their cellars, the Sun's radioactivity being attenuated by walls and thwarted by layers of earth. It was, however, necessary to be lodged in buildings equipped with sufficiently deep cellars; this was not the case for the poorer classes and the mobile population. This is why deplorable excesses occurred; makeshift crews of diggers were not content to excavate subterranean shelters; they laid bare water and gas pipelines in order to take possession of the pipes, producing floods and explosions. Troops had to use force to limit the damage.

Fortunately, this convulsive period of incoherent individual efforts did not last long. Analogous scenes, more or less violent, having unfolded in all countries, the course of everyday transactions almost came to a standstill, and it was absolutely necessary to plan and then construct the necessary means of safe circulation from one state or region to another, as well as coming and going within the bounds of an individual city.

In the first place, a large number of locomotives and carriages were armored with thick sheets of lead, and the companies did their best to reduce traffic by day and increase nocturnal traffic. The crowding of the rails resulted in a series of nocturnal bottlenecks and accidents. The first consequence of the measures taken was, therefore, a transport crisis. Little by little, as they say, things piled up.

Maritime traffic was also slowed down considerably—even more so than terrestrial traffic, at least in the early days. As it was not possible for ships only to cross the oceans by night, it was necessary to bring all transoceanic vessels successively into dry dock, in order to cover their decks in layers of lead sufficient to protect the passengers. For some vessels this work changed the height of the flotation line and, in consequence, their stability, so it was necessary to modify their construction. Submarines were used for short journeys and for coastal trade, but they did not win the favor of the public. The attraction of protection by lead was such that, when one ship foundered, the story went around that a rich upstart who had had a suit made out of lead fabric, flatly refused to take it off; he buckled his lifejacket over the top of it and, when he came into contact with the waves, inevitably sank like a stone.

Such were the first incidents of international circulation. They were reiterated for some time, but the cities adapted rapidly. Four days after the great revelation, lead fabric hats, coats and cloaks were already to be found in the stores, as well as lead gloves and footwear. That was, however, only a stopgap measure, firstly because the hastily-fabricated garments and accessories were only of use to people of medium build, and secondly because, even in themselves, they represented such a weight that walking, or any movement at all, became extremely difficult. The hats weight about three kilos, as much as a veritable helmet, and the seven-kilo boots nailed feet to the sidewalk. The attire of a deep-sea diver, in the capacity of an "antiradioactive suit" became what a smock and trousers had formerly been to a workman, aerial everyday wear. Such costumes were, however, the privilege of the rich; the poor found themselves deprived. The result of that was the pillaging of boutiques, which was violently repressed.

The Government, very agitated, resolved to take general measures—but it did not know exactly what to do. Fortunately, its task was alleviated thanks to a Senor Lopez, a Spanish umbrella-merchant. The said Lopez had an idea, simple in principle, but which was deemed a stroke of genius and enjoyed spectacular success: the idea of a leaden parasol, which he named the "pararad."

This portable shelter ensured a relative protection— but the pararad was found to be somewhat impractical, for, constructed in haste on a massive scale, it could not be closed; it was, in sum, a heavy and voluminous mushroom, under which it was, strictly speaking, possible to walk along the street but which occasioned serious annoyance indoors. As it was larger than a single-batten doorway, it greatly complicated the business of passing from one room to another, and the spectacle of several members of the same family coming and going through their apartment under pararads, complaining and cursing when they met, was painfully comical. Besides, one entire category of human beings, even in the highest ranks of society, could not be equipped with them: children.

In fact, the manufacturers had not yet had the time to produce small pararads; the large ones were too heavy, and dragged down their terrified slender carriers when they fell. Babies also remained unprotected, for it was most uncomfortable to support a nursling and a pararad at the same time. To humanity's shame, some women abandoned the former in favor of the latter. A makeshift provision was devised: children under six were drawn along in small carriages covered by lead awnings, and they were maintained indoors beneath little lead-leaf roofs, and forbidden to move. This prohibition, which prevented them from engaging in their customary play, brought about an unprecedented epidemic of infantile melancholy.

An entire mass of living beings was still endangered, however: animals. They were interesting to the extent that they were useful to humans; it was therefore necessary to protect beasts of burden, farmyard animals and livestock.

The Chamber experienced stormy sessions. They began, of course, by covering the Bourbon Palace, the Senate, the Elysée Palace, the Banque de France and all administrative buildings with impenetrable leaden carapaces, the lives of administrative personnel being, in their eyes, the most precious of all. It was, however, also necessary to think about safeguarding that of the nation, especially in the persons of its soldiers and its children, for representatives without a nation no longer represent anything but themselves—which is to say, not very much, relatively speaking.

All the available lead was, therefore, requisitioned by the State, and the trusts had to surrender it. It was realized a little later that it would have been expedient to tax them before effecting the requisition, and long debates began in national assemblies in relation to that tax, without reaching any conclusion.

Meanwhile, the authorities did not remain inactive; taking inspiration from the pararad model, they ordered the construction of huge shelters equipped with leaden cupolas, underneath which markets could be held. They lead-lined hospitals, subsidized theaters and schools—but the protection of houses remained the responsibility of individuals. A multitude of lawsuits was launched between tenants and landlords, each party imputing to the other the duty of protecting rented accommodation and paying for that protection. In addition, some buildings collapsed, because they were unable to support the supplementary weight of the lead that had been abruptly inflicted upon them.

A question of equal gravity was that of lighting. To garnish windows with lead was to suppress light. The leaded glass from which radiologists' eyeshields were constructed was certainly available, but in very small quantity and at an extremely high price. Human beings enclosed in dark places during the day therefore illuminated their environments for several weeks with artificial light, which resulted in an excessive rise in the price of means of lighting. In this interval, an Italian chemist, Doctor Finoli, discovered the formula of a glass opaque to radioactivity but translucent; it was a silicate of lead, thorium and tin obtained by the fusion of specific fractions of pure sand, red lead, thorianite and stannic dioxide. The glass in question only permitted a blurred vision, but it permitted the revival of sunlit indoor existence. At the same time, the factories began to produce vast numbers of thin lead sheets cut to size, which served to paper the walls of continually-inhabited rooms, and the government introduced a wise measure; in order prevent monopolizers from covering more rooms in lead wallpaper than they needed to live, they instituted a ration-card giving each person the right to 4.9 square meters of protection, with a premium for numerous families—which was very popular. The system functioned well, save for a certain amount of black marketeering.

At the end of the day, however, social life mostly takes place outside private dwellings, so the clothing industry, under the pressure of necessity, made astonishing progress. Fabrics were woven rapidly in all colors—but all those colors, mixed with lead, retained dark shades, giving entire costumes a metallic aspect of the strangest effect.

Good tailors produced bespoke clothing not deprived of a massive elegance. For men, the initial fashion was for long raglan overcoats, bowler hats with broad curved brims that marked the face and neck from the Sun, lead gauntlets to hide the wrists and canvas shoes, for it had not been possible to combine lead and leather. For women, there were ample cloaks and hats of every shape profoundly enclosing the head—and it was rather amusing to see light ornaments, such as feathers, tulle and lace surmounting such heavy headgear.

It is also necessary to relate that headaches became endemic, especially among people obliged to circulate in confined spaces and travel underground, as on subway trains. In truth, nothing was more irritating than feeling crushed by the heat and the weight of clothing that was entirely unnecessary during the subterranean journey—but where and how could cloakrooms be installed? By virtue of that fact, underground railways lost a large fraction of a clientele that they had, on the contrary, expected to increase, since subterranean journeys offered full security. Reality often takes responsibility for giving the lie to the most logical inductions in such a manner.

If journeys in the open air regained favor, however, sedentary work in the same conditions was abandoned, as far as possible, for it was more agreeable to work underground, in the costumes of the past, than above ground in the new armor. That is why the jobs of sewer-workers miners and tunnelers became highly sought-after by the working classes; among commercial employees there was a marked preference for working in basements. These preferences resulted in considerable perturbations of wage-scales, in consequence of abrupt and frequent strikes. As it was necessary, though, in the final analysis, to seek work where it was to be found, the conditions of proletarian existence were not greatly modified.

On the other hand, that of the leisured class was completely transformed. Its members almost never went out any more by day; social life became primarily nocturnal. Elegant beauties could not reconcile themselves to putting on such heavy apparel. They remained seated or lying down until nightfall beneath magnificent lead awnings provided by their admirers; in cases of urgency they climbed into armored automobiles and were driven to the shops or pleasure spots by chauffeurs liveried in lead. The fashion was established of going to dinner in the cellars of fashionable restaurants; there, amid wine-racks full of bottles sparkling in the illumination, between varnished tuns and hogsheads, on carpets of fine sand, refined guests sat down before the most delicate foodstuffs, not without having selected for themselves, directly from the racks—that was the fad of the moment—the wines that they would drink.

In the streets, the general appearance of passers-by, which had at first been that of pachyderms, gradually became, thanks to the ingenuity of tailors and couturiers, that of gigantic insects: cloaks of every sort, very ample and darkly metallic in color, resembled the wing-cases of enormous beetles, especially among women, who further emphasized the resemblance with hats whose feathers were similar to antennae and thin legs similar to the feet of scarabs.

Automobile omnibuses were reminiscent of the military vehicles that had been named "tanks". Horses, whether in harness or mounted, were caparisoned in "plumbite," a thick leaden cloth that was solid and not very costly. Dogs—cherished pets, at least, were walked entirely covered in little leaden cloaks with four sleeves, which protected their bodies and limbs but had the inconvenience of inhibiting their capers. All in all, the general aspect of the streets, as much by virtue of the dark envelopes of living beings as by the leaden cladding of houses, became sad and grey.

Certain buildings, however, remained deprived of all protection longer than the rest: military barracks. Administrative formalities, projections, estimates and all sorts of conditions routinely slowed down the placement of protective sheathing. At the same time, a committee was studying the alternative project of a leaden uniform, which was followed by several others. The scientists were thus able to study at their leisure the subsequent effects of "radiopathy" on the soldiers: extreme irritability, intense anemia, loss of strength, disturbances of vision, loss of hair—including eyelashes, eyebrows and beards—and acute erythema, often accompanied by lesions in all the parts of the body exposed to solar radiation.

To ward off these disastrous consequences, all permissions compatible with concerns of national defense were granted. Military personnel were thus able to take shelter among civilians. One arm of the military gave the authorities particular anxiety: the cavalry. How could their mounts be maintained in a serviceable state?

Mounted regiments were urgently reassembled in wine-growing regions, and the horses sent down into the immense cellars of the great producers. In the final count, the administration paid up for a million leaden helmets and cloaks, of a model that recommended itself by its heavy warrior-like grace.

The Ministry of Agriculture found itself facing problems at least as worrying. In the majority of communes, the insouciant peasants were not taking any protective measures. It required the balding and death of numerous animals to force their owners to utilize the lead sheets deposited in the town halls by the care of the prefects. Another question remained to be resolved; it was not only a matter of conserving the animals, but also their feed. Now, the herbage was perishing; the meadows once green and lush, were turning brown and developing immense bare patches, and the naked red earth presented the appearance of wounds in the scorched earth.

The destruction of vegetation constituted the worst disaster of all, for without plants, there would be no more animals, and without animals, no more humans. The idea that seemed the most practical was to build frameworks over large areas that could be roofed with leaded glass, and gather the livestock in these "sheltered pastures". Under the leaded glass the meadows survived; everywhere else, they stopped growing, and then began to die. As for the trees, there was no remedy. Thus, with the summer barely begun, an autumnal landscape was already in the process of dying—or, rather a landscape that was rugged, bleak and burned in appearance, as in the approaches to large deserts. It seemed that a leprosy issued from the abyss was slowly eating away the terrestrial flesh, all the way down to the stones that were its bones.

In the savage countries, the decimated populations embarked on merciless slaughter, everyone attributing the scourge to the malice of his neighbors. The policed nations were less inclined to accept it as destiny, and gradually contrived, by the solidarity of research and effort, to thwart its cruelty—but existence had become ponderous and grey. Humankind had been happy during the Age of Gold, active during the Age of Silver, bellicose during the Age of Iron. Now it became neurasthenic—and that was the Age of Lead.

XI. A Radiological Idyll

It would, however, be an exaggeration to claim that the whole world was unhappy. To begin with, those enriched by the scourge—the "leprosy profiteers," as some newspapers called them—almost all led an ecstatic life of feasts, balls and orgies. Then there were the philosophers, for whom the calamity formed a precious subject of meditation; the believers, to whom it appeared as an ordeal imposed by Heaven and necessary to salvation; and the men of science of every category, who "laid"[28]—according to the technical expression—communications of every sort. There were also those in love, for love, "invincible in combat," triumphs over all enemy forces.

Among the latter, amid the general distress, Winnie and Monsieur Galfo flourished. It will perhaps be remembered that the ravishing American had been overtaken by a sudden and immoderate taste for research in radiophysics. Entirely devoted to his speculations on the Bourse, Barcklett had left her completely at liberty, according to the transatlantic fashion. Winnie, therefore, frequented the young man's laboratory assiduously. Utterly disgusted with literature, she had enrolled at the Faculty of Sciences as an honorary auditor, purchased an intimidating stack of radiological treatises, and remained for long hours in her "scientific home," according to her

---

[28] This metaphor does not translate; the French *pondre* (from the Latin *pono*, to lay) is used literally to mean "to lay an egg" but is also used metaphorically to mean "to write [creatively]," when the writing process in question is imagined to be awkward.

own exquisite expression. There, she examined the apparatus, admired everything, and understood nothing.

Galfo found her adorable. Furthermore, alone with him, the young woman was scarcely at risk, either from the viewpoint of honor or that of health. Galfo was too honest a fellow to take the slightest liberty with regard to a woman, even a pretty one, without express encouragement; that eventuality being realized, Galfo was capable of protecting his laboratory and apartment fully. Barcklett had furnished him with an imperious superfluity of lead—it was the least he owed him. Thus, an idyll was secured between teacher and pupil, among various instruments, the names of which she asked with an apprehensive and curious smile.

"Oh, dear master, dear friend, will you tell me what that pretty little copper apparatus is, which resembles a photographic apparatus?"

"A spectroscope, Winnie."

"What is it for?"

"For examining the solar spectrum."

"Oh! I'm afraid!"[29]

"Don't worry. 'Spectrum' means a colored image of all the shades of the rainbow or a soap-bubble."

"I can look at it then?"

"Of course. Put your eye to that objective. The vertical stem is directed at the Sun. Can you see the lines of the spectrum?"

"Oh! How pretty it is! The ribbon of Iris! What about the Galfo rays—can I see them?"

---

[29] This joke doesn't translate either; Winnie has misunderstood "*spectre solaire*" [solar spectrum] as "solar spectre."

"Certainly. Look to the left, at those dazzling red radiations, as if the shade were intended to evoke the profound burns that they cause…"

"Oh! Frightful! Show me something else…"

"This is a spectrograph. It's not sufficient to see the lines of the spectrum; it's necessary to conserve the trace. My spectrograph measures them and, by virtue of the adaptation of photographic apparatus, fixes the in black and in color. Look at this collection of prints…"

"Oh! Marvelous! Oh, dear Stéphane, how I love radiophysics! Show me more. There—what's that?"

With their fingers, and sometimes their arms, enlaced, they strolled tenderly over the rubber-lined floor of the laboratory…

"That, Winnie, is a radiosclerometer, which measures the penetration of radioactive rays; their penetrative force is appraised automatically by reading the graduated scale in front of which that little needle is moving. And this is Wilson's electrometer…"

"Our president?"

"No, but a man just as great. The electrometer is designed to register radiation; a gold leaf gets further away from or closer to this polished copper disk."

"Oh! Splendid! And all this works?"

"In normal conditions, marvelously. Presently, all my apparatus becomes worthless as soon as solar light reaches it, so it's all protected."

"And this?"

"That's FitzHerald's polaristroboscope[30]… and here's the Coolidge bulb, the empress of bulbs, which

_____

[30] I have been content to contract Falk's "Fitz Herald" rather than substituting the likelier FitzGerald, because I cannot find any evidence that the Irish physicist George FitzGerald (1851-

permits the production of a quantity of X-rays unknown until today. American genius, you observe, has given rise to astonishing progress in radiophysics."

"Oh, how polite you are to tell me that, dear Stéphane!"

"Dear Winnie!"

A kiss united their lips—and if he tension and attraction of their souls could have been measured in units of electrical force, it would doubtless have sent the needle of the Thomson electrodynamometer crazy. They therefore made a mutual promise to unite themselves in the bonds of matrimony, and Winnie immediately started planning the furnishing of a leaden nest where their protected happiness might curl up amorously.

A shadow fell upon the scene, though; when Winnie revealed her intentions to Barcklett, the latter reacted as he would have done to a traveling salesman of sewing-machines.

1901) invented anything that might be called a "polaristroboscope." The latter word does, however, produce one hit on Google, from a document presented to the Académie des Sciences, so Falk was not the first to coin it and might well have appropriated it from elsewhere. "Radiosclerometer" is also not unknown, although Falk presumably improvised that one for the purposes of Galfo's imagined research. With regard to subsequently-mentioned apparatus, the new light bulb developed for General Electrics by William Coolidge was distinguished by its use of a "ductile tungsten" filament and did not produce abundant X-rays. William Thomson (later Lord Kelvin) did patent an electrodynamometer, although the invention is generally credited to Werner von Siemens, and Galfo would surely have had a more recent model.

"You can't marry that unprepossessing scientist, whose exact worth is my $5000—assuming that he still has them."

"He's worth every penny that he's earned for you, Papa."

"You're talking sentiment, child, and I'm talking business. It's not the same language."

"My language is that of the heart, Papa. Stéphane doesn't even have your $5000 any longer, for he spent them on sweets and cream cakes for me. He's a gallant man."

"A mighty imbecile. He'll never get rich. Making a deal without assuring himself of a percentage of my profits was a costly omission. The daughter of the Lead King can't marry the Prince of Fools."

"She will marry him."

"Don't count on it. I've got a magnificent match for you: the son of the Iced Fruit King…"

"He can drown himself in one of his vats!" cried Winnie. "I don't want your ices—I want my Galfo!"

He being stubborn and she obstinate, agreement was problematic.

"If that's the way it is," he concluded, "we're going back to Philadelphia on the next steamer."

XII. A Business Dinner

Sitting in the drawing-room of a sumptuous hotel, Winnie was smoking a cigarette dreamily. Barcklett was reading the evening papers. It was only 2 p.m., but as the wireless telegraph did not work by day, the major evening dailies had brought forward their printing times.

"There's a very interesting article in the Times," he told his daughter, "entitled *What of the Planets?* The reporter writes: *Astronomical observations reveal that solar radioactivity is not only affecting the Earth. Thus, Mars has changed color; it was red and has become green. The vegetation covering its surface, which formerly had a carmine-poppy tint, has doubtless been subject to Galfo radiation, for it has faded and withered, changing to the most lamentable greenness.* You ought to read it, having become a 'scientist'..." And he uttered a little snigger, which was apparently unwelcome, for his daughter turned her back on him, blowing out cigarette smoke forcefully.

"Ah! Ah!" Barcklett went on. "The run on the 'Winnie' is still going on. Your name had brought the mine good luck. I'll order further prospecting."

Without replying, the young woman looked out of the window, at a lower-class wedding procession: the traditional landaus were rolling slowing along, their thin horses fatigued by their leaden caparisons; as the weather was magnificent, the hoods were open, and seen room above, the entire wedding-party—groom, bride, relatives and guests—resembled a series of big bells set in pairs on the benches. The bride was only identifiable by the veil of classic muslin covering her lead hat; the couple's black-gloved hands were joined…

The young American sighed, and turned to her father. "Are you still brutally inflexible?"

"It's marvelous," he replied. "I no longer know how much money I have. The government's promising taxation. It will promise it until the end of the world—that's perfect. What?"

A gilt-edged hotel bellboy brought a folded piece of paper on a sliver tray.

"For you, Winnie," said Barcklett. "A telegram."

She opened it and read:

Beloved darling!

I have just made an immense discovery. Can you come to the laboratory? My cousin Parmesif, who is with me, swears that our happiness is guaranteed. Come quickly, I beg you.

She rang, and the bellboy reappeared.

"My car."

The bellboy bowed and disappeared.

"Are you going out, Winnie?"

"Yes."

"We're dining at eight, don't forget—we're going to the Opéra. I'm going to the Club now."

He rang. The bellboy reappeared.

"My car."

The bellboy bowed, and disappeared.

Twenty minutes later, Winnie was listening, with great delight, to Galfo's revelations.

She threw her arms around his neck. "I had a presentiment of something good, darling! You must dine with us…Monsieur Parmesif too. And the three of us will—how can I put it?—*have Papa where we want him.*"

"The situation is delicate in one respect," Parmesif opined. "Your father won't promise anything without reasoned explanations—and once the explanations have been given, will he still promise?"

Winnie replied, haughtily: "Papa has many faults, but he has the greatest quality of all: he's honest."

"That is also," Parmesif replied, gallantly, "the greatest of skills."

"For now," said Winnie, "I shall telephone my father to tell him that I'm bringing two guests."

Around a brightly-lit, flower-laden table, three guests in suits and the charming Winnie were consuming a choice meal. The tender flesh of admirable pullets swelled out, superabundantly stuffed with truffles.

Winnie launched the attack with vigor and simplicity. "Papa!"

"My child?"

"What do you say to this news: Monsieur Galfo is capable of making you sudden millions, or impoverishing you so sternly that we would be almost ruined?"

Galfo blushed. Parmesif smiled graciously. Barcklett, with his fists set solidly on the table, scarcely frowned, and replied: "That's certainly news. Well, if it can be proven, I'll offer Monsieur Galfo…"

"Your daughter, Papa?"

"No."

"Then he'll keep quiet, and you'll be ruined. You'll keep quiet, my love!"

"Yes," Galfo replied, coughing with emotion.

"May I be permitted, Monsieur," Parmesif put in, "to point out that my cousin Galfo is from an excellent family, that, in spite of his youth, he is famous, and that his science will one day…"

Winnie interrupted him. "Monsieur Parmesif, it's necessary not to discuss sentiment with Papa. Instead, dictate the terms of an agreement…"

"Very well," Parmesif went on, without seeming disconcerted—for the interruption had been planned in advance—"I propose to Monsieur your father the following formula: 'If Monsieur Galfo makes me a profit of so many dollars, I promise to give him my daughter.'" Addressing himself to Barcklett, he added: "That profit should be matched, I think, by a similar sum paid to my cousin."

"What profit?" asked Barcklett. "I want a million dollars, minimum."

Winnie shrugged her shoulders. "Make the contract out for two million, Papa—you see that we have nothing to fear. I add that if you refuse, dear Galfo will say nothing to you, but will talk to others—and the others will have you where they want you. There you are."

"All right," said Barcklett. "Two million. I'm listening. Talk."

"Very well, Monsieur," Galfo declared, in a voice whose assurance he tried to maintain. "Sell all your lead immediately. Tomorrow, its value will go down; the day after, it will go down even further, and within a week, it will be worthless."

"Why?"

"Because your stocks will become unnecessary, because the cruel Sun will become our benevolent Sun again, returning progressively to its normal activity."

"How? Explain!"

"This is how it is. After having observed an increasing perturbation of my measuring apparatus, and having tracked that effect to its maximum, I observed a few days ago that instead of continuing its ascent, the curve had rapidly turned downwards. It tended to become parallel to the time axis on the diagrams on which I inscribe the phenomenon on an hourly basis. Finally, this very morning, my measurements showed that the decrease of penetrating radiation is quite clear; the curve is declining slowly toward the abscissa."

Galfo fell silent. The American looked at him. After a moment's reflection, he replied: "I don't understand any of that—but it's not your explanation that's important: it's the fact."

He scribbled figures in his notebook, then shook Galfo's hand, saying: "Take my daughter. I'm off to the telephone."

XIII. Epilogue

The nightmare that had weighed upon the world gradually vanished. A month after Galfo's prediction, the Sun had lost all radioactivity and lead almost all its value. That sad metal took a long time to resume its normal course. Nevertheless, the effects of the scourge persisted among the afflicted organisms. A large number of human beings, until they died, no longer knew any but a diminished, painful life complicated by such accidents as dyspepsia or failing eyesight. A deficiency of white blood corpuscles became the rule among all those who had not protected themselves sufficiently; they were recognizable by their waxy pallor.

In sum, it is incontestable that an entire generation was sacrificed, to varying degrees—but what is a generation in the sequence of centuries? A wrinkle that is born, propagates and dies on the infinite and moving sea of time.

Of all the heroes of the faithful preceding narrative, only Monsieur Saumaître, the Lieutenant-Governor's elegant secretary, who had been ordered to remain at his post, was profoundly affected; the Galfo rays produced certain devastating consequences in him. Completely sterilized, the honest man decided not to marry the woman he loved, and languished and died shortly thereafter in the accursed Gabon, which he had never left. The sad end of that worthy official was, however, compensated by his superior's good fortune; Monsieur Parmesif received in France the high distinction that he might never have obtained far from the metropolis and nearer to the Sun; named Officier de la Légion d'Honneur, he was also promoted to the office of Governor of a lovely colony. To complete his happiness, his wife's hair grew again, sufficiently for her to wear a bob.

Galfo went to live in the United States, commissioned by the American government to set up the largest radiophysics laboratory in the world. Winnie became Madame Galfo. Barcklett, a manifest billionaire, now adores his son-in-law.

The moribund plants gradually recovered their vigor and beauty. All the creatures of nature rejoiced in concert, finally liberated from their burdensome terror—except for the fish, which the scourge had not attained, and which remained, in consequence, strangers to the universal delight.

The Age of Lead was over, well and truly finished. It was then that the military administration finally started distributing a million lead uniforms and helmets...

SF & FANTASY

Guy d'Armen. *Doc Ardan: The City of Gold and Lepers*
G.-J. Arnaud. *The Ice Company*
Aloysius Bertrand. *Gaspard de la Nuit*
Félix Bodin. *The Novel of the Future*
André Caroff. *The Terror of Madame Atomos*
Didier de Chousy. *Ignis*
C. I. Defontenay. *Star (Psi Cassiopeia)*
Charles Derennes. *The People of the Pole*
Harry Dickson. *The Heir of Dracula*
Sâr Dubnotal *vs. Jack the Ripper*
Alexandre Dumas. *The Return of Lord Ruthven*
J.-C. Dunyach. *The Night Orchid. The Thieves of Silence*
Henri Duvernois. *The Man Who Found Himself*
Henri Falk. *The Age of Lead*
Paul Féval. *Anne of the Isles. Knightshade. Revenants. Vampire City. The Vampire Countess. The Wandering Jew's Daughter*
Paul Féval, *fils. Felifax, the Tiger-Man*
Arnould Galopin. *Doctor Omega*
V. Hugo, Foucher & Meurice. *The Hunchback of Notre-Dame*
O. Joncquel & Theo Varlet. *The Martian Epic*
Jean de La Hire. *Enter the Nyctalope. The Nyctalope on Mars. The Nyctalope vs. Lucifer*
G. Le Faure & H. de Graffigny. *The Extraordinary Adventures of a Russian Scientist Across the Solar System* (2 vols.)
Gustave Le Rouge. *The Vampires of Mars*
Jules Lermina. *Mysteryville. Panic in Paris. To-Ho and the Gold Destroyers*
Jean-Marc & Randy Lofficier. *Edgar Allan Poe on Mars. The Katrina Protocol. Pacifica. Robonocchio. Tales of the Shadowmen* (anthos.; 6 vols.)
Xavier Mauméjean. *The League of Heroes*
Marie Nizet. *Captain Vampire*
C. Nodier, Beraud & Toussaint-Merle. *Frankenstein*
Henri de Parville. *An Inhabitant of the Planet Mars*

Polidori, C. Nodier, E. Scribe. *Lord Ruthven the Vampire*
P.-A. Ponson du Terrail. *The Vampire and the Devil's Son*
Maurice Renard. *Doctor Lerne. A Man Among the Microbes.
The Blue Peril. The Doctored Man. The Master of Light*
Albert Robida. *The Clock of the Centuries. The Adventures of
Saturnin Farandoul*
J.-H. Rosny Aîné. *The Navigators of Space. The World of the
Variants. The Mysterious Force. Vamireh. The Givreuse
Enigma. The Young Vampire*
Brian Stableford. *The Shadow of Frankenstein. Frankenstein
and the Vampire Countess. The New Faust at the Tragicomi-
que. Sherlock Holmes & The Vampires of Eternity. The Stones
of Camelot. The Wayward Muse.* (anthologist) *The Germans
on Venus. News from the Moon*
Kurt Steiner. *Ortog*
Villiers de l'Isle-Adam. *The Scaffold. The Vampire Soul*
Philippe Ward. *Artahe*

MYSTERIES & THRILLERS

M. Allain & P. Souvestre. *The Daughter of Fantômas*
Anicet-Bourgeois, Lucien Dabril. *Rocambole*
A. Bisson & G. Livet. *Nick Carter vs. Fantômas*
V. Darlay & H. de Gorsse. *Lupin vs. Holmes: The Stage Play*
Paul Féval. *Gentlemen of the Night. John Devil. The Black
Coats: The Cadet Gang. The Companions of the Treasure.
Heart of Steel. The Invisible Weapon. The Parisian Jungle.
'Salem Street*
Emile Gaboriau. *Monsieur Lecoq*
Steve Leadley. *Sherlock Holmes: The Circle of Blood*
Maurice Leblanc. *Arsène Lupin: The Blonde Phantom. The
Hollow Needle. Countess Cagliostro*
Gaston Leroux. *Chéri-Bibi. The Phantom of the Opera. Roule-
tabille & the Mystery of the Yellow Room*
William Patrick Maynard. *The Terror of Fu Manchu*
Frank J. Morlock. *Sherlock Holmes: The Grand Horizontals*
P. de Wattyne & Y. Walter. *Sherlock Holmes vs. Fantômas*

David White. *Fantômas in America*

SCREENPLAYS

Mike Baron. *The Iron Triangle*
Emma Bull & Will Shetterly. *Nightspeeder. War for the Oaks*
Gerry Conway & Roy Thomas. *Doc Dynamo*
Steve Englehart. *Majorca*
James Hudnall. *The Devastator*
Jean-Marc & Randy Lofficier. *Royal Flush*
J.-M. & R. Lofficier & Marc Agapit. *Despair*
Andrew Paquette. *Peripheral Vision*
R. Thomas, J. Hendler & L. Sprague de Camp. *Rivers of Time*

NON-FICTION

Stephen R. Bissette. *Blur 1-5. Green Mountain Cinema 1*
Win Scott Eckert. *Crossovers* (2 vols.)
Jean-Marc & Randy Lofficier. *Shadowmen* (2 vols.)
Randy Lofficier. *Over Here*

HEXAGON COMICS

Franco Frescura & Luciano Bernasconi. *Wampus 1*
Franco Frescura & Giorgio Trevisan. *CLASH*
 Luciano Bernasconi, Jean-Marc Lofficier & Juan Roncagliolo
Berger. *Phenix 1*
Claude Legrand, Jean-Marc Lofficier & Luciano Bernasconi.
Kabur 1
Franco Oneta. *Zembla 1*
Lina Buffolente, Jean-Marc Lofficier & Jean-Jacques Dzia-
lowski. *Stangers 1: Homicron*
Danilo Grossi. *Strangers 2: Jaydee*
Claude Legrand & Luciano Bernasconi. *Strangers 3: Starlock*

ART BOOKS

Jean-Pierre Normand. *Science Fiction Illustrations*
Raven Okeefe. *Raven's L'il Critters*
Randy Lofficier & Raven OKeefe. *If Your Possum Go Daylight...*
Daniele Serra. *Illusions*